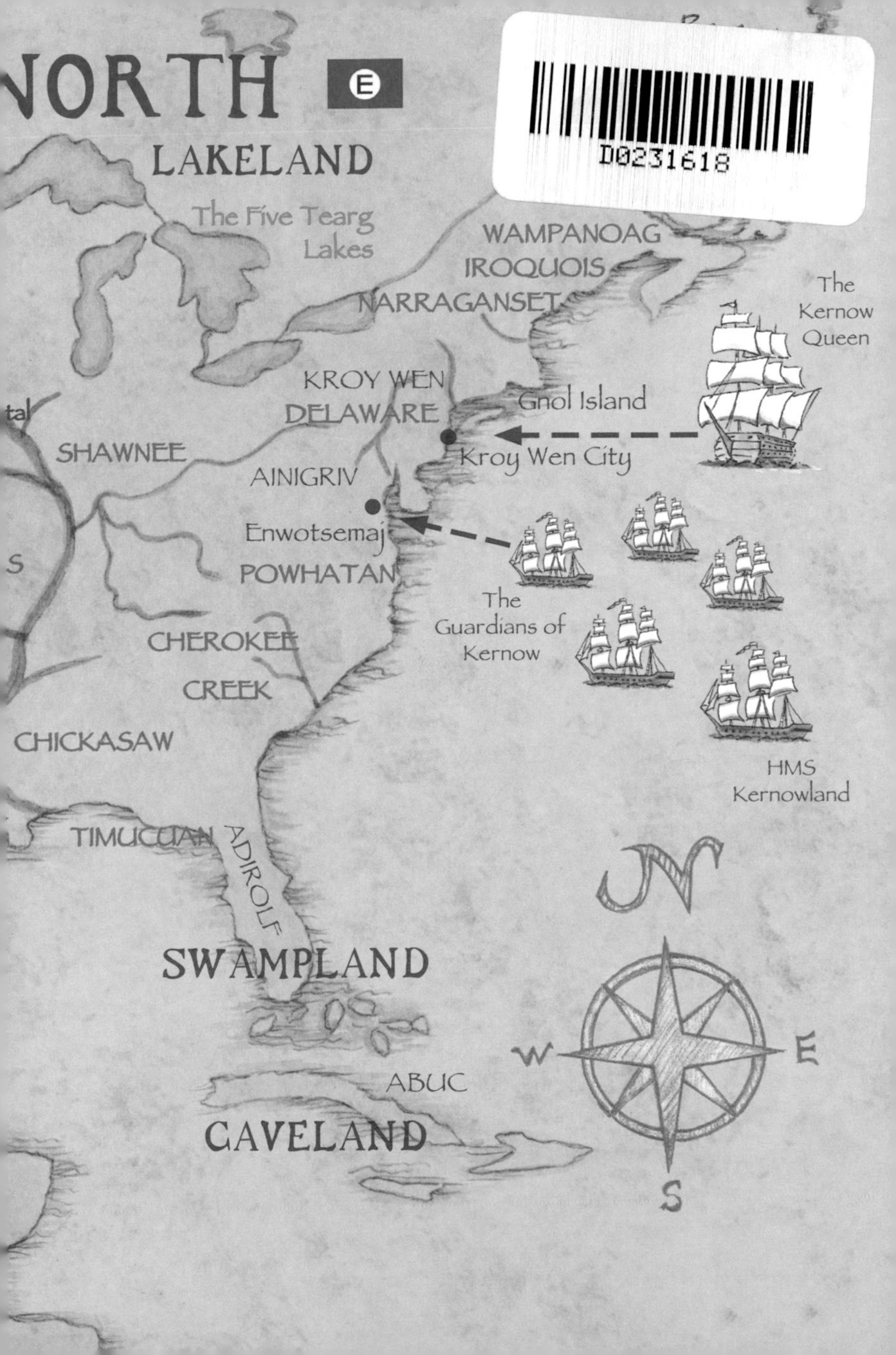
NORTH
E
LAKELAND
The Five Tearg Lakes
WAMPANOAG
IROQUOIS
NARRAGANSET
The Kernow Queen
KROY WEN
DELAWARE
Gnol Island
SHAWNEE
Kroy Wen City
AINIGRIV
Enwotsemaj
POWHATAN
The Guardians of Kernow
CHEROKEE
CREEK
CHICKASAW
HMS Kernowland
TIMUCUAN
ADIROLF
SWAMPLAND
W
E
ABUC
CAVELAND
S

Kernowland

Slavechildren

Book Five

Titles available in the Kernowland series:

Kernowland 1 The Crystal Pool
Kernowland 2 Darkness Day
Kernowland 3 Invasion of Evil
Kernowland 4 Pigleg's Revenge
Kernowland 5 Slavechildren
Kernowland 6 Colosseum of Dread

To our darling granddaughter,
Olivia.
Merry Christmas
All our love
Nanny + Bamps

Kernowland

Slavechildren

Jack Trelawny

CAMPION BOOKS

A catalogue record for this book
is available from the British Library

ISBN 978-0-9546338-9-9

Campion Books is an Imprint of Campion Publishing Limited

Illustrations by Marlene Keeble
and Louise Hackman-Hexter

Printed and bound in the UK by
CPI Antony Rowe, Chippenham SN14 6LH

Reprinted 2011

First published in the UK in 2009 by

CAMPION BOOKS
2 Lea Valley House, Stoney Bridge Drive,
Waltham Abbey, Essex, UK EN9 3LY

www.kernowland.com
www.erthwurld.com

For Tizzie and Louis

Illustrations:
The front cover illustration and the front endpaper
were produced by Marlene Keeble.
The illustrations of Tizzie and Louis, and the back endpaper,
were produced by Louise Hackman-Hexter.

AUTHOR'S  NOTES

Apart from Tizzie & Louis,
the characters and events in this book
are entirely fictitious.

In the *Erthwurld* books,
'Erth' means 'Earth',
and 'Wurld' means 'World'.
Evile is pronounced *ee-vile* to rhyme with mile.
Skotos is pronounced *skoh-toss* – it means 'darkness' in Greek.
Photos is pronounced *foh-toss* – it means 'of light' in Greek.
Graph means 'draw' in Greek, so a *photograph* is...
'a picture drawn with light'.

Websites
There is lots of other information
as well as clickable zooming maps
on the Kernowland and Erthwurld websites

www.kernowland.com
www.erthwurld.com

ONE

The Green Gas Explosion

CLOUBOOOOOOOOOOOOOOOOOOOOOM!

A huge explosion reverberated around Crosstrails Clearing.

A cloud of green gas spread out in all directions from the blast centre, enveloping every living being within a fifty-pace diameter in a murky, pea-green fog.

Everyone and everything – children, rescuers, beasts – fell to the ground the moment the gas reached them.

Even the leaves on the trees drooped from the effects.

The tree octopus that enfolded Tizzie immediately loosened its grip as it succumbed.

'TIZZ…'

The terrified young girl thought she heard the sound of her brother's voice as a bright green flash went off inside her head.

She dropped to the ground.

Thddd!

Her head hit the jungle floor with a thud.

TWO

Dragged Away

'TIZZZZIEEEEEEEE!'

Louis shouted his sister's name as he heard the green gas explosion.

Gurt was carrying him away down the South Trail as the pirates hurried from the Crosstrails Clearing as fast as they could go.

'NOHHHHHHHHH!' Louis shouted again, desperate to help Tizzie as he watched her slump to the ground, with the tree octopus enfolded around her.

Louis wriggled and writhed and just managed to get his toes onto the jungle floor.

'LET ME GO!' he protested, as he swung his leg and kicked Gurt in the shin as hard as he could.

'Gurrhhhh!'

Gurt gurgled.

But the struggle was futile.

Pigleg's punisher was far too strong for him.

The brutish pirate tightened his vice-like grip and dragged Louis away as if he were no more than a rag doll.

THREE

'I *Want* To *See* My *Sister*'

'I *want* to *see* my *sister*,' groaned Louis again, still wriggling and kicking as Gurt snatched him up and threw him over his shoulder like a sack of potatoes.

'Gurrhhhh!'

The punisher gurgled again as he picked up the pace down the trail.

'No chance,' growled Purgy, who was now huffing and puffing along beside Gurt at the back of the line of marching pirates.

'But she could be hurt,' protested Louis, as the clearing full of green gas disappeared into the distance.

'That's as maybe,' puffed Purgy again.

'But I'd advise you to do as you're told, lad, or there'll be big trouble for you... I say, big trouble.

'Come quietly or the Cap'n will make sure you're sorry.

'And I mean... very sorry!'

FOUR

'Drop It!'

As he gave up struggling on Gurt's shoulder, Louis was suddenly aware of the crumpled Godolphin Map in his top pocket.

Then he thought he heard a voice, just like Misty's, speaking inside his head:

'The map. It's important. Drop it!'

Could it really be his little friend talking to him?

Whether the voice was real or not, Louis decided to act.

Very slowly and carefully, so that Gurt wouldn't notice, the brave young boy brought his hand up so that his thumb and forefinger could grip the map.

He was just able to pull the parchment out of the pocket before letting it drop.

He watched the map fall amongst the twigs and leaves on the trail.

FIVE

Smelling Crystalsalts

Tizzie regained consciousness.

There was a strange smell in her nostrils.

Her eyes were itching but they wouldn't open.

'All is well, Princess, you are with friends,' said Clevercloggs. His was an unfamiliar voice but its gentle kindness was very reassuring.

'I'm... I'm not a princess...'

'She's still delirious,' said Clevercloggs to Mr Sand, as he continued to hold a tiny muslin bag under Tizzie's nose.

'Yes,' agreed Mr Sand. 'But she'll be fine in a short while. You get on with waking up the others with your smelling crystalsalts, and I'll look after Princess Tizzie.'

Clevercloggs nodded in agreement before removing a mask from his face and returning it to his rucksack. Whilst his Clevergas had incapacitated every other person and thing in the clearing in an instant, the little white mask had protected him from its effects.

After a few more moments, Tizzie was able to open her eyes.

'Ah, there you are,' said Mr Sand. 'Now, don't be frightened, all is well, you are with friends.'

His voice and face were familiar, and Tizzie felt even more reassured.

SIX

Kidnapped By Pigleg

'I know you're still sleepy from the effects of the Clevergas,' said Mr Sand, 'but you must listen carefully. I have been helping your brother, Louis, so please trust me.'

'*Louis*...' said Tizzie, still groggy but quickly regaining her senses when she heard her brother's name.

'What's happened to him? Where is he?'

'I'm afraid he's been kidnapped by Pigleg.'

'Ohnaohhhhh,' groaned Tizzie.

She knew what *that* was like.

'But if we're to have any chance of rescuing him,' said Mr Sand in a very serious tone, 'you must pretend to be a princess, just as your brother is pretending to be a prince.'

The look on Tizzie's face showed she wanted to know more.

SEVEN

Princess Tizzie

Mr Sand quickly told Tizzie the same thing he had told Louis all that time ago back at the Polperro Inn.

He and the King had made up a story about her and Louis being from Forestland and of royal blood.

This was to stop anyone finding out about the Crystal Pool and, they hoped, would give them the best chance of sending the two children home safely.

Mr Sand finished his story with a warning: 'It is so important that you do not reveal who you are or where you are really from.

'Otherwise, there will be so many awkward questions and the story will be so sensational that everyone will know about you in no time.

'Your brother is very good at being a prince...

'Do you think you can you be a princess?'

Tizzie soon saw the importance of what was being said, and agreed to do as Mr Sand asked.

'Yes, I'll try my best,' she said.

Mr Sand looked very pleased and handed Tizzie a rolled bundle of clothes. She went behind a tree, removed her rags, and put the new garments on over her swimming costume.

Whilst Clevercloggs was waking others up with his smelling crystalsalts, the Chief Surveyor and Mapmaker then told Tizzie as much as he could about her cover story and how she should behave as a princess.

EIGHT

Misty Helps

Clevercloggs had been busy with the bag of smelling crystalsalts from his rucksack.

The little gnome had only revived the Bulubaa, the rescuers, the children from the hold… and, of course, Misty, the little blue mouse.

He certainly didn't want to wake the tree octopuses up!

When he had brought little Lucy back to consciousness, Clevercloggs immediately noticed that she was very ill.

'Looks like she's delirious with the airalam fever. This is a job for you, Misty.'

With that, the gnome took the little blue mouse from his pocket and placed him gently near the big red lump on Lucy's arm. Misty knew what to do. The healing blue mist formed around him as soon as he started twitching his whiskers. The nasty red lump started shrinking immediately. Within minutes, Lucy was feeling much better.

Misty then busied himself healing all those who had been injured. After Misty had helped everyone who needed it, Clevercloggs spoke again.

'We must get away from here before the effects of the Clevergas wear off and all these fearsome creatures wake up.'

'Yes,' agreed Mr Sand, 'and we need to see if we can rescue Prince Louis from the clutches of those awful pirates before *The Revenger* leaves Nwotegroeg.'

NINE

A Sad Parting

At the edge of the clearing, by the start of the South Trail, Clevercloggs spoke again in a very serious tone.

'This is where we need to split up. A smaller group will be able to travel much quicker to rescue Louis. And we can't take the little ones on this mission. The Bulubaa have agreed to take all of you young children to safety. There is dangerous work to do and we cannot risk you being captured by Pigleg's pirates again. Tizzie and Jack will come with us. Masai and Hans, we would be grateful if you would go with the children and look after them as if you were their big brothers and try to make sure they all get back to their homes around Erthwurld. Until that is possible, at least you will all be safe for now with the Bulubaa.'

Hans and Masai wanted to go to help fight the pirates and rescue Louis, but they understood that Clevercloggs was very wise and agreed to do as they were asked.

It made Tizzie very sad to part from all her friends.

'Goodbye, Hans. Goodbye, Masai.'

A little tear welled in her eye as she hugged each friend in turn. She knew she might never see them again. But she also knew the parting was necessary if they were to have any chance of rescuing Louis.

And so it was that a small band of heroes set out down the trail going as fast as they could: Clevercloggs, Mr Sand, Princess Kea, Jack, Tizzie… and Misty the little blue mouse.

TEN

The Sea Guardians of Kernow

To Bella Bodella, it seemed like such a long time since she and the other dolphineers had boarded the Kernish Navy ships that had been ordered to retreat from the invasion of Kernowland and regroup in Acirema North.

After an arduous voyage across the Citnalta Ocean, the torn and battered warships of the Sea Guardians of Kernow were finally limping towards Ekaepasehc Bay, the largest estuary in Acirema North. It was on the mid-eastern coast, in the state of Ainigriv.

As they sighted the bay, Bella reflected on her situation. What changes there had been in her life in the few short weeks since she had been crowned 'Miss Towan Blystra' in a beauty contest. Now she was an officer in the Kernish Navy who had taken part in the Battle for Kernowland… and killed a trog!

Bella looked over the side of the ship to check on Dash. Her dartingdolphin, and those of all the other dolphineers, had swum alongside the ships throughout the whole voyage. She was proud to think that she had played her part in making sure there would be a dolphineer force ready, willing, and able to one day help reclaim her homeland from the Empire.

Bella waved to Dash, who replied by diving under the water and shooting up into the air before doing a back flip and splashing down again. She smiled warmly at his antics.

Then her thoughts returned, as they so often did, to her boyfriend, Cule Chegwidden. Had he survived the invasion?

ELEVEN

The Kernow Queen

Cule Chegwidden had worked his passage to Acirema North on the merchant vessel, *The Kernow Queen*. The boat was heading for Kroy Wen City on the north-eastern coast of the continent.

As he swabbed the deck, Cule couldn't help thinking about the events that had led him to be on this vessel.

After killing the Emperor's favourite trogs, he counted himself very fortunate to have escaped from Kernowland with the help of his friends and neighbours. Their help had ensured that he could now fight on and at least have a chance of one day freeing his homeland from Evile's tyranny.

As he thought about the loyalty of those who had helped him, and their refusal to give him away even under sustained interrogation by Evile's forces, he was reminded just what he would be fighting for: the cause of Good and Right.

But, like the other members of RAE who were fighting against Evile all over Erthwurld, he was well aware he couldn't do battle with the Emperor alone. Working together was essential if they were to be able to defeat the Empire. His weapons were safely stowed in his rucksack under his hammock. Now he just needed to get to Acirema North and find and join the rebels.

Cule's other constant thoughts were for his special girl, Bella. He hoped and prayed that she had made it safely through the invasion battle.

TWELVE

The Bouncing Sack

Gurt had dumped Louis back on the ground some time after they had left the clearing.

He was now being force-marched down the trail.

Grunter's head was in a bloodstained sack being pulled along a few paces ahead of him.

Louis had heard one of the pirates say it was needed as proof of the pigmonster's death.

So that Captain Pigleg could collect a reward.

The mutant boar's head was so heavy it had to be dragged by two men.

The sack was bouncing along the track.

It jumped into the air a little every time it hit a stone or root.

One of the pigmonster's sharp tusks had made a hole in the sack.

The tusk created a groove in the ground as the head was dragged along.

Blood seeped through the hole and into the groove so that the bouncing sack left a dark red stream in its wake.

Despite this gruesome sight just ahead of him, Louis was unmoved.

He was a much tougher kid now than the innocent young boy who had entered Echo Cave all that time ago.

THIRTEEN

The Piece Of Parchment

Tizzie knew that they had to get to Nwotegroeg quickly if they were to save Louis.

Brushing away her tears, she put her best foot forward to follow Cleverclоggs.

As she did so, she stepped on something.

Bending down to pick it up, she saw it was a piece of parchment.

'That looks familiar,' said Mr Sand, glancing knowingly at Cleverclоggs as he spoke.

'It does indeed,' replied Cleverclоggs.

Mr Sand put out his hand.

Tizzie handed the piece of parchment to him.

'Well, I never. This is a very important find.'

Cleverclоggs seemed very pleased too.

'Well done, Princess Tizzie.'

'But what...?' began Tizzie.

'We'll explain later,' said Mr Sand, as he put the parchment safely away in his pocket.

As they set off down the trail again, Tizzie was amazed at the speed with which Cleverclоggs could move on his sticks.

Although she tried to think of other things, she found herself constantly wondering what was on the parchment.

But she couldn't possibly have known just how important it would prove to be.

FOURTEEN

The Big Little Cleversack

On the way down the trail, Mr Sand spoke to Tizzie quietly, telling her more about Kernowland, Jungleland, and the rest of Erthwurld. She learned all the things that would help her play her role as Princess Tizzie, including that she should address her mentor as, 'Sand', rather than 'Mr Sand'. She tried to listen and learn as much as she could because she knew the smallest bit of knowledge could be important in the rescue of Louis.

That evening, they stopped for a short rest.

'We won't sleep tonight,' said Clevercloggs. 'That way we may be able to catch up with the pirates. But we must take some time to eat and gather our strength.'

With that, he took a can and a big saucepan from his rucksack.

That little backpack just doesn't seem big enough for everything that's in there, thought Tizzie.

'That Cleversack is a wonder!' said Mr Sand admiringly.

'It certainly is,' said Clevercloggs. 'Don't know what I'd do without it.'

Tizzie watched with interest as Clevercloggs emptied the powdered contents of the can into the saucepan.

'I'll get some drinking water,' said Princess Kea.

Within minutes, Kea returned with the life-giving liquid.

Tizzie watched again as Clevercloggs poured the water into the saucepan. The powder fizzed immediately.

Then it started spitting and puffing.

FIFTEEN

The Godolphin Map

In no time at all, the fizzing, spitting, puffing powder in the saucepan had expanded into a bubbling stew.

It was just enough food for everyone.

To Tizzie's complete surprise, it was very tasty…

And piping hot!

'Tseeep!' 'Tseeep!' 'Tseeep!'

'Waaarp!' 'Waaarp!' 'Waaarp!'

'Vvit!' 'Vvit!' 'Vvit!'

'Hoahoah!' 'Hoahoah!' 'Hoahoah!'

'Cheweeweewee!' 'Cheweeweewee!' 'Cheweeweewee!'

'Yuuuur!' 'Yuuuur!' 'Yuuuur!'

Tizzie hungrily devoured her rations, whilst listening to the Jungleland Dusk Chorus as the birds and the beasts of the jungle joined each other in welcoming the night.

It was then Mr Sand's turn to speak as he brought the piece of parchment from his pocket.

'Now, before we set out again, it is important that we all know certain things. It looks like Prince Louis had the good sense to drop something very important for us to find.'

'What is it?' asked Tizzie.

She was now itching to know.

'It's a Godolphin Map.'

SIXTEEN

The Red Wand

'This is a very special map,' said Mr Sand, as he opened the piece of parchment. 'It was made by the powerful magic of Godolphin the Great.'

Tizzie leant forward to look at the map.

She loved *anything* to do with magic.

'I learned about these maps in lessons,' said Jack. 'Only a few were made. They change to show the country you are in.'

'Indeed they do,' said Mr Sand. 'Is that all you know about them?'

'Yes,' said Jack.

'Is there more?' asked Tizzie.

'Oh, much more,' continued Mr Sand. 'This map has great secrets to reveal in the hands of a Rainbow Wizard.'

'As long as the wizard has one of these,' added Clevercloggs, as he reached into his Cleversack.

'A Red Wand!' exclaimed Jack.

'Yes, YOUR wand,' said Clevercloggs.

'But, where? … how?' said Jack. 'Did Reddadom give it to you?'

Clevercloggs glanced at Mr Sand, as if to say… you tell him.

SEVENTEEN

What *Has* My Brother Been *Up To*?

'I'm afraid I have some bad news,' said Mr Sand.

'Reddadom is dead.'

'*Dead...*'

Jack's head dropped as he heard the terrible news about his teacher.

The Chief Red Wizard had been like a kindly uncle to him.

'Yes, I'm afraid so,' continued Mr Sand.

'Murdered in a cowardly fashion.

'Violothan has turned traitor.

'He tricked all the other Rainbow Wizards at the White Light Ceremony...

'And attacked them with *Skotos*.'

'The Death Stone?' queried Jack quietly, still reeling from the sad news he had just heard. 'I thought it was just a legend.'

'I'm afraid not,' said Mr Sand. 'I was there and saw the terrible destructive power of the Dark Beam with my own eyes.

'Princess Tizzie's brother, Prince Louis, was there too.

'It was only due to his quick thinking and brave actions that we escaped with our lives.

'He was a hero.'

Louis, a *hero*?! thought Tizzie.

What *has* my brother been *up to*?

EIGHTEEN

The Hidden Crystals

Tizzie decided not to interrupt by asking what Louis had been doing. She'd find out more later. For the moment, she listened carefully as Jack spoke again.

'But I still don't understand how you have my wand.'

'Well,' began Mr Sand, 'as you know, between classes and ceremonies, all the wands of red apprentice wizards were kept by Reddadom. Because you were absent, your wand was on his person when Violothan attacked.'

'But we have friends at Kernow Castle,' added Clevercloggs. 'Pemberley the butler is the bravest of men. He risked his life to take this wand. I asked him to retrieve it in case we found you. In the confusion, nobody noticed it, possibly because there was one wand for every wizard they buried. Pemberley just managed to purloin it before the other wands were all gathered up and taken by Violothan. Perhaps he and the other traitors assumed you took yours with you when you disappeared.'

Mr Sand now spoke again in a very serious tone: 'You are the last of the good Rainbow Wizards, Jack. The last person alive who can help us find all the eight crystals of the *Amulet of Hope*, the only weapon that has any chance against *Skotos*.'

'But I thought the eight crystals of the *Amulet* were lost,' said Jack.

'Not lost… ' answered Clevercloggs, pausing for a moment as he spoke... 'hidden.'

NINETEEN

Godolphin's Hope

'Hidden?' queried Jack.

'Yes, hidden for safe-keeping by Godolphin the Great,' said Mr Sand.

'Scattered across the eight continents of Erthwurld,' added Clevercloggs. 'It was Godolphin's most fervent hope that one day a Rainbow Wizard would be born who would have enough of the Three Qualities to find the Seven Rainbow Crystals and *Photos*; and wield the *Amulet of Hope* in one final battle against Devillian and his Forces of Darkness.

'But how can I do it?' asked Jack, 'I'm just an apprentice.'

'Yes, that is true,' agreed Mr Sand. 'And I must admit, young man, we thought the same thing at first. But then we realised that, since – apart from Violothan – you are the *only* Rainbow Wizard left alive, you are the last person in Erthwurld who can possibly fulfil Godolphin's wish. If Erthwurld is to be saved, it is *you*, Jack Truro, who must find the Rainbow Crystals and *Photos*, and bring them together in the *Amulet*.'

'And then,' added Clevercloggs, 'you must learn to wield the *Amulet of Hope* – the most powerful weapon you can imagine – in the cause of Good and Right.'

'Yes,' confirmed Mr Sand. 'And if you are to have any chance of defeating Violothan and *Skotos* in the battle we are planning, you must quickly discover how to use the *Amulet* to activate *Photos* and produce the Bright Beam.'

TWENTY

'*Golow An Mappa*'

Tizzie looked at Jack with a mixture of admiration and concern. She could see in his face that he was at the same time proud and worried in equal measure… as if his task were both a huge honour and a great burden.

Mr Sand spoke again in an urgent tone. 'Only time will tell if you are the Wizard of The Hope. For the moment, we have more pressing concerns. Let's get back to the map. As a young wizard you learned to reveal that which is hidden to the eye with your wand and the correct spell said in Kernewek, the language of Rainbow Magic. Is that not so?'

'Yes, we learned it in Year One.'

'Do you remember how to do it?'

'Oh yes, we practised it all the time.'

'Good,' said Mr Sand. 'To reveal what is hidden here, you need to say, "light the map" in Kernewek.'

Jack was a very good student. He had done very well in his Kernewek studies. He pointed his wand at the Godolphin Map and spoke in what Tizzie thought must be a special spell voice.

'*Golow an mappa*.'

Tizzie and the others watched. At first nothing happened.

Mr Sand shared an anxious glance with Clevercloggs.

Then, after a few more anxious seconds, a point of red light began to glow faintly and blink on the map.

It was blinking in Acirema North.

TWENTY-ONE

The First Rainbow Crystal: Red

'Tipi City!' exclaimed Princess Kea, as she saw where the red light was blinking on the map. 'I've always wanted to go there.'

'I'd have guessed as much,' mused Clevercloggs, exchanging a knowing glance with Mr Sand. 'Godolphin would have put the First Crystal of the *Amulet* in a very safe place.'

'And you couldn't get much safer than Tipi City,' added Mr Sand. 'That's about the farthest you could get from Evile's clutches.'

'With this wand we should be able to find all seven of the Rainbow Crystals for the *Amulet of Hope*,' said Clevercloggs.

'It looks like the map will show us the location of one stone at a time... starting with the red one.'

TWENTY-TWO

You'll Need All The Help You Can Get

'But I thought it was the main stone from the centre of the *Amulet* that could be activated to produce the Bright Beam,' said Jack. 'Couldn't we just try to find *Photos*?'

'Yes, we could,' agreed Mr Sand.

'But the seven Rainbow Crystals give the *Amulet* extra power.

'They would boost the strength of *Photos* in any battle against *Skotos*. It would be much better if we could find them.'

'I'm sure you don't need reminding,' added Clevercloggs, 'that you are still an apprentice, whilst Violothan is a powerful and experienced Chief Wizard.

'Which means if you are to have any chance of defeating the Dark Wizard and his Dark Stone...

'...you'll need all the help you can get.'

TWENTY-THREE

The White Wand

'And, there's something else we've had to consider,' continued Clevercloggs, in a sombre tone. 'We cannot begin to search for *Photos* for the moment, because, in order to reveal the whereabouts of *Photos* on the Godolphin Map, we need Godolphin's White Wand.'

'Unfortunately, the wand and the empty *Amulet* are held in a secure cabinet in Godolphin's Chamber at Kernow Castle,' said Mr Sand. 'Our friends at the castle are working on a way to get the Wand and the *Amulet*. That won't be easy as the room is under constant guard. They must wait and choose the right time.'

'But even if we can acquire the White Wand,' said Clevercloggs, looking again at Jack, 'we still need a Rainbow Wizard with enough of Godolphin's Three Qualities to be able to wield it.'

'Yes,' confirmed Mr Sand, 'using a Red Wand is one thing… but using Godolphin's White Wand is something else entirely.'

All eyes were on Jack as Clevercloggs continued.

'But we can think about all this again later.

'For now, if we're going to have any chance of rescuing Prince Louis, we should be on our way to Nwotegroeg before the pirates take him away on their ship.'

TWENTY-FOUR

The *Questers*

'I think we should have a name for our little band,' said Clevercloggs, as they set out down the South Trail.

'Oh I agree,' said Mr Sand. 'It always helps to have a team name.'

'The *Rescuers*?' offered Princess Kea.

'Hmm, that's good, but not quite right.'

'The *Heroes*?' suggested Jack.

Nobody seemed to think that was ideal.

'How about the *Questers*?' said Tizzie. 'Because we're on a quest to find the hidden Rainbow Crystals.'

'Marvellous.'

'Splendid.'

Everyone nodded and agreed.

'And I suggest our team motto should be, *Onen hag Oll*,' said Clevercloggs.

'Good idea,' agreed everyone again, before Mr Sand spoke in an urgent tone.

'Now, *Questers*, let's get to Nwotegroeg as quickly as we can.'

TWENTY-FIVE

The Importance Of Louis' Key

Clevercloggs reminded the *Questers* of something very important as they made their way down the jungle trail.

'As well as rescuing Prince Louis, we must retrieve his Golden Key before it gets into the hands of Manaccan and the other traitors.

'If they can open the lock tile, they'll be able to get down into the Golden Cavern and use the Crystal Door.'

'Yes,' added Mr Sand, 'I dread to think what Evile would be able to do with the Crystal Door if he gained access to it.

'Can you imagine if he and his evil cronies were able to travel around Erthwurld in an instant?'

'It would increase his power enormously,' said Clevercloggs.

'He would be able to crush RAE in no time at all.

'So we must stop Evile getting hold of Louis' Golden Key at all costs.'

TWENTY-SIX

'Pigglyleggy!'

Pigleg had decided that the pirates wouldn't sleep on their journey down the South Trail.

So they made very good time.

When they arrived back at Nwotegroeg, Big Bessie was there in the street to greet her man.

'Piggyleggy!'

She was very pleased he had survived the fight with Grunter.

'Ah, there's me big cuddly girl!' said the Captain, as he gave Bessie a hug. 'How's your grandma?'

'Very ill, I'm afraid. I'll have to stay here to nurse her. I just wanted to see you were alive and well, and to tell you I'm staying behind for a while.'

'Okay,' said Pigleg. 'But I'm afraid we can't tally long, my sweet. We've got work ta do.'

'See you soon then, Piggy.'

'I'll miss ya.'

After Captain Pigleg had said his gooey goodbyes to his girlfriend, he led his men straight to the Jungleland Inn.

TWENTY-SEVEN

A Very Good Spy

Joyous Jilla was at the inn, serving all the customers and being very jolly as usual.

The wily old woman was a very good spy. None of the pirates would ever have guessed from her manner that she was watching them all very carefully and recording everything she saw with her photographic memory.

'Here Cap'n,' she said with a big smile, 'have some more rum.'

'Don't mind if I do,' said Pigleg. 'And make sure it's a *laarrge* one.'

Joyous poured rum into Pigleg's glass until it reached the top and spilled over down the sides.

'Now that's what I call a double ration,' roared Pigleg, as he downed the glassful in one swig. 'Another of the same, if you please, landlady. And I'll have a double ration for each of me shipmates as well.'

'Two cheerrs for the Cap'n,' shouted one of the pirates.

'Hip, hip, hooree!'

'Hip, hip, hooree!'

Whilst Pigleg and his men enjoyed their rum, Louis was made to stand in the middle of the inn.

'Look at the floor and mind your manners,' ordered Purgy.

After what seemed like ages, Louis saw the hoof stepping towards him on the wooden boards of the inn.

Click, thud. Click, thud. Click, thud.

TWENTY-EIGHT

Confiscate Everything

'I suppose you've got some nasty ideas about killin' me or one of me mates on this voyage, Assassin Boy?!' spat Pigleg as he approached.

Louis was unsure as to what to say or how to act.

He just continued to look at the floor.

'So what murderous weapons have you got in your Assassin's Toolkit then?' shouted the pirate leader, as he put his hook under Louis' chin and pulled the boy's head upwards.

'Nothing,' said Louis defiantly.

'Well, he's got some spirit, I'll say that for 'im, eh mates?' said Pigleg, with more than a hint of admiration for the young killer before him.

'Aye, Cap'n,' said the pirates in unison.

'So we'll be taking no chances. He'll not be murdering me, nor any of me crew. Not now. Not ever. Not if I can help it, anyway.

'Mr Cudgel, I want you to confiscate everything the boy has on him. Otherwise we won't be able to rest easy in our hammocks, will we lads?'

'Nay, Cap'n,' agreed the pirates in unison.

'Purgy, you heard the Cap'n,' barked Cudgel.

Purgy now seemed wary about approaching Louis on his own.

He motioned to Gurt to step forward towards Louis first, before issuing an instruction.

'Turn out your pockets and give your stuff to me.'

TWENTY-NINE

A Key Of Gold

Louis reluctantly turned out his pockets.

He knew it was futile to resist when he was surrounded by so many pirates.

Purgy seemed very pleased with the first item he confiscated.

'Ah, what have we here? A key of gold, I say a key of gold.'

'Shall we melt it down straight away, Cap'n?' asked one of the crew, as he looked longingly at the key and tried to work out his own share of its worth as a lump of pure gold.

'Not just yet, Skalliock,' answered Pigleg. 'We'll get back to Wonrekland and see if it's of any value to the new king as a key for turning a lock.

'If not, we can melt it down and sell it as treasure.'

The next item to be taken from Louis was his Kaski.

'Ah, now there's a special knife indeed,' said Pigleg, recognising the Kaski as something very valuable.

'Probably what he does most of his killin' with. Worth quite a few evos anywhere in Erthwurld, eh mates?'

'Aye, Cap'n,' agreed the men.

Everyone knew the value of a Kernish Army Knife.

THIRTY

A Small, Strong Chest

Louis' catapult, ammo belt, and compass were taken from him and put on the table.

The young boy watched with dismay as all his prized possessions were confiscated and, one by one, transferred to a small, strong chest.

The last thing to be put in the chest was the Golden Key.

Pigleg picked it up and studied it carefully, noting the clear crystal at the end.

'I've a feeling this will be something the King of Wonrekland will pay handsomely for,' said the pirate shrewdly. 'I wager it opens an important lock.'

With that, Pigleg placed the Golden Key carefully on top of the other items.

Then he locked the chest and put its small bronze key in his pocket for safekeeping.

Louis was careful to make a note of which pocket the bronze key was in, just in case he got the chance to take his things back.

'Now, let's get back to the ship, mates,' said the pirate captain.

'We've got two rewards waiting to be collected.

'A big one for the pig's head...

'And an even bigger one for the Assassin Boy.'

THIRTY-ONE

Shackle Him Well

The pirates walked back to *The Revenger*, with Mr Cudgel carrying the small chest containing Louis' confiscated things.

Louis watched Cudgel take the chest into the Captain's quarters.

Then Pigleg gave orders for him to be put in the hold.

'And make sure you shackle him well... or some of you may be found with your throats cut in the morning.'

Louis put his foot on the first rung of the ladder, just as Tizzie had done all that time before him.

However, on descending into the hold, unlike his sister, he found no other children to greet him and share his sorrow.

Shackles were fastened around his wrists and his ankles.

He was then chained securely to a beam.

'Cap'n's orders,' said Purgy, warily, almost apologetically, as if he was just a little scared of Louis' reputation as a vicious and dangerous assassin.

Then the tattooed pirate left the little boy in the hold.

Up on deck, Louis heard Captain Pigleg bark out the order to set sail for Wonrekland.

Once again, he was all alone with his thoughts and worries.

His main concern was, as ever, for his sister.

Had Tizzie been seriously hurt – or even worse – by that hairy creature or the green gas explosion in the clearing?

THIRTY-TWO

Louis Was Gone

The *Questers* arrived at the outskirts of Nwotegroeg just as *The Revenger* was sailing away.

Louis was gone.

Mr Sand confirmed there was no chance of rescuing him from the ship.

'We'll have to wait until he gets back to Kernow Castle.'

'Oh, Louis,' sighed Tizzie. She was very worried about what would happen to her little brother now. She knew just what it was like to be held captive in the hold by the pirates, and she could only imagine what the new king and those other nasty people she had been told about were going to do to him when he was delivered into their hands.

'Yes, and I'm afraid it will be a long time before the ship arrives back home,' added Clevercloggs, looking sympathetically at Tizzie, as if he could sense her concern for her brother. 'Great patience is required of us sometimes, I'm afraid.'

'Should we find out what the local members of RAE know about all this?' asked Kea.

'My thoughts precisely,' agreed Mr Sand.

They waited until dark.

Clevercloggs then left a note for Joyous Jilla behind the Jungleland Inn as before.

He collected a reply note a little after midnight.

Her report carried two very important items of news.

THIRTY-THREE

A Great Powwow... This Morning!

'Joyous says Pigleg has possession of the other Golden Key,' said Clevercloggs as he read the reply note. 'He confiscated it from Louis at the inn, and intends to sell it to Manaccan.'

Everyone agreed this was very bad news indeed.

On a very different subject, Joyous had heard through the rebel network that a Great Powwow would take place at Tipi City in Acirema North.

And Clevercloggs was expected to be there as it was he who had suggested that the powwow be convened in his note to Chief Natahwop.

'When is the meeting?' asked Kea.

'Today,' replied Clevercloggs. 'This very morning, in fact.'

'This morning!?' exclaimed Jack. 'But it's lunchtime *now*; we've missed it.'

'But isn't Ameri... I mean... Acirema North behind Acirfa in time?' asked Tizzie, remembering from her school lessons that the sun rises in the east and sets in the west. 'It's still very early morning there.'

'Very good, I'm glad someone listens in school,' said Mr Sand, at the same time looking at Jack as if he should have known that.

'We must get to Tipi City right away to attend the Great Powwow,' said Clevercloggs in an urgent tone.

'I sincerely hope we're not too late.

'The future of Erthwurld depends on it.'

THIRTY-FOUR

Travelling By Golden Key

Clevercloggs destroyed the note from Joyous Jilla.

Then he removed the spare Golden Key from his pocket and held it up in the air.

'Time to go back to the Golden Cavern. Travelling by Golden Key is simple if you follow the rules.'

Tizzie was excited and scared at the same time. Would travelling back to the cavern be like travelling through the Crystal Pool? She knew she would soon find out.

'Now,' said Clevercloggs, 'Princess Tizzie, you put your hands on my shoulders. Then the others will do the same behind you, so that we're all lined up and ready to travel back to the cavern.'

Tizzie did as instructed. Then she felt Princess Kea's hands on her shoulders. Jack was behind Kea. Then Mr Sand was right at the back.

'Make sure you hold on tight,' said Clevercloggs.

He then bent down and put the crystal end of the Golden Key on the ground before saying: '*Golden Cavern, by the power of Godolphin.*'

In that same instant, Tizzie felt Clevercloggs being stretched downwards, as if he were being pulled by the key into the ground. Her hands still gripping his shoulders, it felt like she was being stretched and dragged into the ground behind him.

She held on tight.

THIRTY-FIVE

Shackled In The Hold

The Revenger sailed slowly back down the River Aibmag towards the sea.

As he lay shackled in the hold, Louis was becoming increasingly concerned as to whether he was ever going to meet up with Tizzie again.

He was also concerned about other things.

It had taken no time at all to travel to Sandland using the Crystal Door.

But how long would he now be on this ship?

If Tizzie and Mr Sand had survived the explosion, did they even know where he was so that they could at least have a chance of rescuing him?

All the worry and the long walk from Crosstrails Clearing to Nwotegroeg had made him very tired.

Eventually he couldn't stay awake any longer.

He closed his eyes and fell into a deep sleep.

THIRTY-SIX

Treasure At Port Lujnab

Whilst Louis slept, the pirate ship made good progress.

Much later in the day, he was awoken from his dozing when he heard a cry go up.

'Cap'n! Port Lujnab on the bow.'

'Arghhh, not long now lads,' said the Captain. 'There'll be treasure waiting fer us there.'

'Hurrahhhhh!' cheered the pirates in unison.

The noisy excitement amongst the pirates woke Louis.

Stuck in the dark and dingy hold, he listened carefully, trying to work out what might be the reason for all the commotion.

It sounded like the Captain was going to the port to collect his reward for killing Big Red Grunter.

Louis continued to listen out for clues as *The Revenger* docked at Port Lujnab.

There was a lot more noise as the Captain and a dozen of his men left the ship.

THIRTY-SEVEN

'Pigleg!' 'Pigleg!' 'Pigleg!'

The Kingchief of Jungleland had been informed of the demise of Big Red Grunter and, to show his appreciation, had sent some soldiers from his personal guard to escort Pigleg and his men to the palace.

He also knew their fearsome reputation and wanted to make sure that the pirates didn't cause any trouble.

As the guards led them through the old part of the town, it appeared to the crew that everyonc in Jungleland had now heard the news.

The blood-soaked sack that Gurt dragged along behind him drew huge crowds along the way.

'Pigleg!'

'Pigleg!'

'Pigleg!'

The people cheered the Captain as he walked.

He waved his hook theatrically in every direction to acknowledge their appreciation.

It was perhaps not surprising that the people seemed very pleased that Grunter was gone.

The pigmonster had, after all, been terrorising their villages and eating their children for many years.

There was a great deal more cheering and hook waving before the Palace of Jungleland came into view.

It stood at the top of a big hill.

THIRTY-EIGHT

Kingchief Banjul

'Magnificent sight, eh lads?' said Pigleg, as he pointed at the large white building they were heading for. 'There'll be some fine treasure in those chests if the palace is anything to go by.'

'Aye, Cap'n,' replied his men in unison.

They entered the palace and were taken into a high-ceilinged room. At one end there was a big throne made of stone, wood, and ivory. A very regal-looking Acirfan man sat on the throne. He wore a huge crown of feathers and ornate precious stones on his head. An announcer stepped forward.

'Silence for Kingchief Banjul of Jungleland!'

'Greetings, Captain,' said the Kingchief.

'Good day, your Chiefness,' said Captain Pigleg, whilst at the same time doing his best to make a little bow. But it was more out of wanting to make sure he would get his treasure rather than any deference to the Kingchief's high position and rank. If the truth were known, the most fearsome and fearless pirate who had ever lived recognised no authority other than his own.

'Now the formalities are out of the way,' said Kingchief Banjul, 'I understand we are to congratulate you for killing the pigmonster.'

'We have indeed done the deed,' confirmed Captain Pigleg, pointing his hook at the bloodied sack containing Grunter's head. 'And we are here to claim the reward.'

THIRTY-NINE

The Severed Head

The Kingchief of Jungleland smiled and clapped his hands.

A guard with a long knife stepped forward and slit open the head sack.

'Ahhhhh!'

'Urghhh!'

'Ooohhh!'

There were gasps and groans from the assembled men and women in the throne room as the enormous, blood-soaked, severed head was revealed for all to see.

The man with the knife studied the head carefully before turning to Kingchief Banjul and confirming the identity of its former owner.

'Grunter.'

The Kingchief smiled a much broader smile and clapped his hands twice.

Two men now hurried in from a side room carrying an ornately decorated chest.

They were quickly followed by two more men with an identical chest.

'Murmurmurmurmurmur.'

A murmuring of excitement spread amongst the pirates as the two chests were set down in the middle of the room.

A key was handed to Captain Pigleg.

FORTY

Two Chests Of Treasure

The leader of the pirates took the key he had been handed, opened one of the chests in front of him, and threw back the lid.

'Whooohhhh!'

There was a stifled gasp from the assembled guests at the sight of the treasure within.

All sorts of coins and jewels and gems twinkled and glistened under the bright palace lights.

'YESSSS!'

The pirates were less reserved in their reaction.

Thud, click.

Pigleg took one pace and put the key in the second chest.

He opened it a crack to check that it too was full of treasure.

He was not disappointed.

'Thank you for keeping your word, your Chiefness,' he said with sincerity.

'We are most grateful for this reward.'

'You have earned it,' said the Kingchief.

'And you are welcome in Jungleland at any time. As long as you promise not to practice your pirates' trade in, near, or around our land and seas.

'That's a promise,' said Captain Pigleg… if somewhat less sincerely.

FORTY-ONE

Operation Pegleg

Once the pirates were back on *The Revenger*, the order was given to set sail for Wonrekland.

As Tugger and Trailblazer pulled the ship into the open seas, and it approached maximum sailing speed, Mr Cudgel spoke to his leader about something that had been planned for a very long time and he knew would be on Pigleg's mind.

'Well, Cap'n, with your share of the Grunter treasure, and the reward for the boy prince, you'll soon be able to have the operation you've been waiting for.'

'Indeed I will, Mr Cudgel,' said Pigleg, 'indeed I will. It's been a mighty long time to wait, but, after we get the five thousand evos reward for that little assassin, I should have enough to pay for the procedure.'

'Marvellous news, Cap'n.'

'Aye,' agreed the leader of the pirates. 'Then this pig's leg will be fused with me own leg... *permanently*!'

'Yes, that'll be much more comfortable for you, Cap'n.'

'Indeed it will, matey. It won't be sore or rub when I walk any more.'

'Oh, that'll be a wonderful thing, Cap'n. I know how you suffer with it.'

'And, make no mistake, Mr Cudgel, I'll not be visitin' any old backstreet bonegrinder. I'm going to get the best mutationeer in the wurld to do it.'

FORTY-TWO

Back In The Golden Cavern

'You *can* open your eyes!' said Clevercloggs with a smile.

Tizzie had closed her eyes when she felt herself being dragged into the ground behind the little gnome.

And she still had them shut!

'I... I thought my head was going to hit the ground,' said the trembling girl as she looked around at the glistening gold and green walls of the Golden Cavern.

'Yes, that's what it feels like the first time,' said Mr Sand from the back of the line. Next time, try to keep your eyes open. The colours you see in the Rainbow Tunnel when you travel by Golden Key are truly spectacular.'

'I kept my eyes open,' said Jack. 'It was brilliant.'

Tizzie was a little disappointed that nobody had thought to mention that she should keep her eyes open, *before* they had travelled back through the Rainbow Tunnel.

Misty now poked his head out of Clevercloggs' pocket.

'I see we're all present and correct,' said Princess Kea, smiling warmly at the little blue mouse as his whiskers twitched in excitement.

'Yes, indeed,' said Clevercloggs. 'And now we must travel with haste to a meeting at which I understand I am expected.'

Everyone linked arms and Clevercloggs put his hand on the Crystal Door: 'Tipi City, Aksarben, Prairieland, Acirema North.'

As it softened, the *Questers* stepped into the green crystal.

FORTY-THREE

Lister's Latest List

Mr Lister was in his office looking at his latest list.

The title at the top of the parchment read: *Slavechildren.*

However, although he was very happy with some of his new lists – such as *Rebels and Troublemakers* – the King's Counterupper was very unhappy with this particular list.

The reason was simple...

It was far too short.

Empty, in fact. Not one name on it.

'Why is it taking the parents so long to decide?' grumbled Lister to Sheviok Scurvy, who was just leaving.

'I felt sure they'd jump at the chance of getting rid of at least one child.

'After all, children are so noisy… and so expensive.'

'Oh I concur most wholeheartedly,' agreed Mr Scurvy, as a trickle of blood slid down his chin and dripped onto the parchment, making a dark red splatter on the title.

'And there's always one child in a family who's naughtier than the others.

'I've often heard parents saying so.'

'So why aren't the parents jumping at the chance to get rid of their naughtiest child?' grumbled Lister.

'Beats me,' answered Scurvy as he left.

'But, whatever the reason, Lester, you'll be in big trouble if you can't get the list completed before the Emperor gets here.'

'I know,' mumbled the Counterupper.

But then his frown turned to a crooked smile as he suddenly thought of an ideal person to help him round up one child from each family.

'I know,' he said, 'I'll get Drym on the case…

'He'll *relish* the job.'

FORTY-FOUR

Spk! Spk! Spk!

Spk! Spk! Spk!

There were three knocks at Lister's door. The Counterupper knew who it was. He'd recognise that rap anywhere... Spikey!

'Ah, Drym,' he said, as he ushered in Wonrekland's newly appointed Slaver-in-Chief. 'Sit down, if you will, I've got something to show you.'

Melanchol Drym sat down and took the rolled parchment Mr Lister handed him.

Drym unravelled the parchment very slowly and deliberately and then leant over to get a closer look.

A nasty smirk formed on his face as he saw the bloodstained title at the top: '*Slavechildren*'.

He knew from the heading what was going to be on the parchment: the name of the one slavechild chosen by each family to comply with *Edict Number I*.

'But where are the children's names?' asked Drym, with a great deal of disappointment in his voice, as he rolled the parchment out further. 'It's already been two weeks and…'

'Yes, I know, I know,' interrupted Lister. 'The parents have had the fortnight I gave them to make their choice.'

'But NONE of them has chosen,' said Drym.

FORTY-FIVE

Drym's Task

'That's right, Mr Drym,' agreed Lister. 'None of the parents has chosen one of their children to be sold into slavery.

'I've been so worried. I can't really *make* them do anything, you see. I'm not an enforcer, I'm just a list maker.

'But then I realised it…

'The solution was there all the time.

'*YOU*, Mr Drym.

'*You* are just the man for the task.'

The nasty smirk on Drym's face grew even wider.

He was somewhat flattered by the Counterupper's confidence in him.

And he immediately began to relish the thought of carrying out the job he was being asked to do.

'I'll have those kids rounded up and on the *Slavechildren* list and in the dungeons waiting to be sold in no time at all, Mr Lister.

'You just see if I don't.

'I'll have whole dungeons full of children before the Emperor arrives… or my name's not, *Melanchol A Drym*.

'I'll get on to it straight away.

'Oh yes I will!'

FORTY-SIX

The Slave Chute

'Ah, *Maggitt & Maggitt,*' sighed Malpas Maggitt as he pointed out his new sign to Mr Drym.

'And a very fine sign it is too, oh yes it is,' replied Drym, as he admired the large lettering above the entrance to the new extension building attached to the side of the Polperro Inn. 'May I offer my congratulations to you both. You've built the auction house in record time.'

'Why thank you, kind sir,' said Mrs Maggitt. 'Now, if you'd like to follow us, we have a lovely surprise for you. We think you'll like it.'

Drym was now both intrigued and excited as the Maggitts led him around to the back of the inn.

Set in the rear wall of the oldest part of the building was a small iron door, at about waist height.

It had a sign above it: *Slave Chute.*

Mrs Maggitt took Mr Drym over to the iron door and pulled at the handle.

Erk!

The door made a low squeaking sound as she opened it to reveal a hole lined with sheets of smooth shiny metal.

'The entrance to the old coal chute,' she informed Drym.

Whsshhhhhhhhhh!

Mr Maggitt dropped a big sack of rubbish down the chute and they all listened as it slid noisily over the metal sheets.

FORTY-SEVEN

Crmmp

Crmmp.

There was a faint crumpling sound as the sack of rubbish hit the hard stone floor at the end of the chute.

Mr Maggitt then spoke again.

'As you know, Mr Drym, we had already made your dungeon down there by converting the old coal cellar.'

'Yes, indeed,' said Drym, 'and splendid it is too, oh yes it is.'

'Then we thought,' continued Mrs Maggitt, almost gleefully, 'that if we repaired the old coal chute, it would be an efficient way of dumping the slavechildren down into the dungeon when they're brought here for storage, before we sell them in the auction rooms.'

'Oh, very good thinking,' said Mr Drym. 'And the slave chute seems to work very well indeed, oh yes it does.

'Can I try it?'

'By all means,' said Mr Maggitt. 'Just imagine it's one of the children you're dropping down there.'

Drym snarled one of his nastiest snarls, imagining he had a small child in his hands as he threw another sack of rubbish down the chute.

The trio of slavers exchanged looks and nods of satisfaction as they heard the sliding and crumpling sounds once more.

Whsshhhhhhhhh.

Crmmp.

FORTY-EIGHT

Drpp! Drpp! Drpp!

'Can I see my dungeon again?' asked Drym, getting excited once more at the prospect of all the fun he was going to have in his new job as Slaver-in-Chief of Wonrekland.

'By all means,' said Mr Maggitt, 'we just wanted to get your approval for the slave chute first.'

The three of them then made their way into the inn and down some steps at the end of a passageway.

They were soon stooping to walk along a dark, narrow corridor, which had long ago been dug out of the ground below the inn. At the end of the short corridor was a cell door, which had a sign above it: *Drym's Dungeon.*

'Oh, it's even more wonderful than I remember, oh yes it is,' said Drym, as he admired the converted coal cellar whilst rubbing his bony grey hands together.

Drpp. Drpp. Drpp. Looking through the bars, he could see and hear water dripping from the rocky ceiling. It was making puddles all over the cold stone floor.

'Don't worry,' said Mrs Maggitt, 'we'll stop that dripping somehow.'

'Oh noohhh!' said Drym. 'No need for that. No need at all. Those kids can put up with a little freezing cold water dripping on to them day and night, oh yes they can. In fact, it'll be good for them. It'll toughen them up for the slave work they'll be doing for the rest of their lives. Oh yes it will!'

FORTY-NINE

The Big Iron Padlock

'Now just look at that new lock, Mr Drym,' said Malpas Maggitt, as he pointed to a huge iron padlock on the door of the cell. 'It would be a clever child who could pick or break that one, don't you think?'

'Indeed it would, Mr Maggitt, oh yes it would,' agreed Drym. 'There'll be no kids escaping from *Drym's Dungeon* in a hurry, oh no there won't.'

The nasty former dustman looked through the bars as he spoke.

Inside he could see the two sacks of rubbish that they'd sent down the slave chute.

They lay crumpled on the floor of the dungeon cell.

'The chute works very well, too,' he said. 'There'll be a few grazes and bruises, but shouldn't be any breakages.'

'Just what we thought, Mr Drym,' said Mrs Maggitt. 'Don't want to damage the goods before sale, do we.'

The trio of slavers exchanged nasty, smug smiles before Mr Maggitt spoke in a very matter-of-fact tone.

'Now, as we discussed before, this dungeon will do as a start, but we need a lot more space for all the slavechildren that will have to be stored down here.'

'Yes,' agreed Drym, before pausing as if in deep thought. 'Have you made plans for the other dungeons?'

Mrs Maggitt answered, with a self-satisfied smirk.

'We certainly have.'

FIFTY

Four More Dungeons

'We're going to excavate the whole of the area underneath the new auction rooms to make four great big dungeons,' said Mr Maggitt proudly.

'Magnificent,' said Drym, rubbing his hands together as he thought once again of all the money he was going to make from his slaving franchise. He then listened carefully as Mr Maggitt continued.

'We're going to extend the corridor and have four more cell doors along it, one for each new dungeon.'

'Yes, and to dig the dungeons, we'll need four giant mole-worms,' added Mrs Maggitt, as if she was relishing the thought of having the gigantic diggerbeasts working there.

'Is their arrival imminent?' questioned Drym, worried that they'd soon run out of cell space in the dripping dungeon when he started rounding up all the slavechildren for Mr Lister.

'Oh, don't concern yourself about that,' said Mr Maggitt. 'They're on the ship and on the way already. They'll be here tomorrow. And then the other four dungeons should be ready in just a few days.'

'Magnificent,' muttered Drym, as he rubbed his bony grey hands together.

'Truly magnificent.

'Oh, yes it is.'

FIFTY-ONE

Zero Tolerance

Wendron was enjoying her new job as Regulator of Schools.

She had been charged with the task of implementing the *Empire Educational Curriculum*, in accordance with *Edict Number IX*. To this end, a new school system had been put in place and was being carefully overseen by the wrinkled witch.

Wendron was explaining her plan to Mr Lister so that he could note it all down for King Manaccan, who would in turn be able to show the Emperor. As Wendron spoke, Lister started yet another new list: *New School System*.

'I've already had the new school uniforms designed,' continued the wrinkled witch. 'In the primary schools the boys have to wear brown shorts and brown shirts, and the girls, brown skirts and brown blouses. All boys and girls will have to wear Evstika armbands.

'We're building a new School Uniform factory at Smogtown,' continued Wendron. 'We'll soon have slavechildren working round the clock producing the uniforms for WENCO. Every family will have to buy the uniforms direct from the factory... and it will bring in a lot of tax revenue.'

'That will please the King *and* the Emperor,' said Mr Lister, who had been making a special note of everything. 'And have you addressed the problem of bad classroom behaviour? I know the Emperor is a stickler for discipline in school.'

'I certainly have,' said Wendron. 'There'll be zero tolerance of naughtiness in my classrooms from now on.'

FIFTY-TWO

WHACKING!

'The Emperor has made a point of saying that naughtiness in the classroom needs to be stamped on… and *hard,*' said Mr Lister. 'Your zero tolerance policy sounds ideal, Miss Wendron. How are you going to achieve it?'

'WHACKING! I've brought back corporal punishment and employed the right people to administer it,' answered Wendron. 'The toughest teachers in the Empire are on their way here, each chosen for their strictness in the classroom. Whacking will be mandatory for badly behaved children. *Six* strokes for a first offence, *twelve* for a second offence.'

'Ouch,' said Mr Lister, with what seemed like genuine concern for the children who would be receiving the punishment. 'Isn't that perhaps a little excessive?'

'Not at all,' said Wendron. 'If you spare the rod, you spoil the child… we all know that! You'll see I've included the costs of two whacking rulers for every teacher in the accounts.'

'*Two* rulers for every teacher?' queried Lister.

'Oh yes, they're bound to break them if they're whacking the naughty children all the time.'

'I see,' said Lister, feeling rather relieved that his school days were finished long ago. 'And the punishment for three offences?'

'For three cases of bad behaviour,' said Wendron, very slowly and menacingly, 'naughty children will find themselves in the slave dungeons waiting to be sold to the highest bidder!'

FIFTY-THREE

Ratphael The Dungeoneer

Drym was waiting excitedly at the dock in Polperro for a very important person to arrive.

Ratphael was a dungeoneer and rattweiler handler.

They said he was the best dungeoneer in the wurld.

He was also a mutant… a *manrat.*

Ninety-seven parts human and three parts rat.

Drym knew that Evile had given instructions for all sorts of mutants to be made by the mutationeers in the laboratories housed in the caverns below Tunnel Rock.

Chewing Creatures and all manner of ferocious beasts were being bred to fight in the colosseums around the Empire.

Other mutants, like Ratphael, had been bred for specialist tasks. In his case he was bred to be a specialist dungeoneer, working in dungeons and keeping control of all the slaves that were being held whilst they were waiting to be sold.

Drym couldn't believe his luck when the Emperor himself had suggested sending Ratphael to Wonrekland to set up the slave dungeons and help train the other dungeoneers.

Drym knew he needed this sort of help. He couldn't afford for any of the children to escape before they could be sold at the slave auctions. He'd be in real trouble if that happened.

The infamous dungeoneer disembarked from the ship that had brought him to Kernowland.

Drym was astounded by what he saw.

FIFTY-FOUR

Rattweilers

Drym stared at Ratphael as he disembarked.

The new dungeoneer was dressed all in black.

He wore a black hat with a very wide brim.

His jaw was much longer than that of an ordinary human. It appeared to be merged with his nose. There were rat-like whiskers at the end of the nose-mouth. He had two rodent teeth at the front of his mouth, which, like rat's teeth, grew continuously. This meant he had to carry a large iron bar on a chain around his neck, so that he could gnaw on it at regular intervals to keep his teeth filed down. He had vivid red eyes – made infra-red by the mutationeers – so that he could see clearly in the dark dungeons of the Empire.

Around the manrat were twelve red-eyed rattweilers – dungeon guardratdogs, known as a 'ratdog pack'. They, too, had infra-red eyes. The red-eyed ratdogs were part rat and part Rottweiler dog. They were squeakbarking viciously. Like their master, they were specialist mutants, bred to be ideally equipped for their work… guarding slaves in dungeons.

The ratdogs were tied to Ratphael by a dozen strong leads. These leads were looped around their necks, with slipknots which strangled them if they pulled too hard. All the leads were attached, at equal intervals, to twelve loops on Ratphael's thick belt.

The squeakbarking ratdogs formed a noisy 'skirt' around their master as he began walking towards Drym.

FIFTY-FIVE

'Dungeons. We Go!'

The long, thick, pink tails of the ratdogs dragged behind them on the dock as they scampered along with their master.

Drym took a few paces towards the dungeoneer and now noticed something very unusual about the manrat. Ratphael seemed to have a large pouch in the back of his trousers, which was hanging down between his spindly legs.

Drym was curious as he was not yet aware that it contained the manrat's own long, pink, curled up, rat's tail.

Ratphael was still gnawing on his toothbar when he got close.

It made a metallic grating sound which sent a shiver right down Drym's spine.

He couldn't bear the sound of metal scraping on teeth.

Drym introduced himself, at the same time stepping forward to shake hands.

'Melanchol Drym, Slaver-in-Chief, Wonrekland.'

'Sqrrrrr!'

Ratchet, the alpha rattweiler, squeakgrowled and bared his fearsome teeth.

Staring into the foaming jaws, Drym saw that the snarling ratdog had two huge rodent front teeth and four long sharp canines. He took a step backwards and withdrew his hand.

Showing no emotion, Ratphael now spoke in a very strange squeaking voice.

'Dungeons. We go!'

FIFTY-SIX

Giant Moleworms

Within minutes of leaving the docks, Drym arrived at the Polperro Inn.

Ratphael was a few paces behind with his pack of ratdogs panting eagerly around him.

Drym introduced the dungeoneer, then quickly realised that he wasn't the only one who had taken delivery of mutants from Empire mutationeers.

On each side of the new auction room were two huge mounds of erth, making four mounds in total.

Sticking out of the top of each mound was a huge, slimy, worm's tail.

Soil was coming out of the ends of each of the worm tails and dropping down the sides of the mounds.

'Giant moleworms, Mr Drym,' said Malpas Maggitt proudly, all the while eyeing Ratphael and his ratdogs with extreme caution.

He had never seen a manrat before, let alone a pack of red-eyed ratdogs.

'Good,' said Ratphael, as if oblivious to the effect he and his rattweilers were having on Mr Maggitt.

The dungeoneer obviously knew about moleworms, but, from the look on his face, Mr Maggitt could see that Drym was none the wiser.

He explained: 'We had four giant moleworms delivered two days ago, Mr Drym.

'They're digging the dungeons beneath the new auction rooms.

'They're mole at the front, worm at the back.

'Living, breathing, excavating machines.

'They tear at the erth underground with their huge claws to soften it up.

'Then they eat the erth and it goes through their wormy bodies and comes out the other end in these mounds on the surface.'

'What about big stones and rocks?' asked Mr Drym.

'They make big piles of them underground,' answered Mr Maggitt.

'Then they push them to the surface with their strong claws.

'We've got four moleworms, one working on each side of the auction room.

'And they work twenty-two hours a day.

'The dungeons should be finished in no time at all with them here.'

'Magnificent new ideas from the Empire, oh yes they are,' said Mr Drym as he viewed the moleworms with appreciation.

'Yes,' agreed Maggitt, 'and they've got ten of them working on the new Conquest Colosseum, along with rhinophants and all sorts of other creatures, so that should be finished in good time for the Emperor's visit as well.'

'Marvellous times to be alive, oh yes they are,' said Drym.

'All good,' said Ratphael again.

'I go below. See underground dungeons now.'

'Oh, of course, Señor Ratphael.'

Having delivered Ratphael to the Polperro Inn, Drym said his goodbyes.

'I must leave you now and get back to the dock at Polperro Port.'

'Are you expecting another delivery today, Mr Drym?'

'I am, Mr Maggitt, oh yes I am.

'Another mutant.

'A working creature to help me round up the slavechildren for sale at the auctions.

'Bred specially for the purpose...

'CHILD-CATCHING!

'Oh yes it is.'

FIFTY-SEVEN

The Rocking Crate

Drym watched from a safe distance whilst a heavy wooden crate was unloaded from a cargo ship on to his old cart.

After the crate had been set down on the cart, the Slaver-in-Chief walked towards the sailor who seemed to be in charge of the unloading operation.

Splck!

As Drym approached, there was a splintering sound and the crate suddenly shifted and rocked a little.

Whatever was inside… was bashing against the sides!

'Watch out,' said the sailor, his hand shaking as he handed Drym the keys to the crate's padlock. 'He hasn't been fed for days.'

'Why not?' queried Drym. 'I gave explicit instructions that he was to be fed regularly, oh, yes I did.'

'That may be so,' answered the sailor, his voice quivering a little. 'But nobody was brave enough to open the feeding hatch.'

Splck!

There was another splintering sound and the crate shifted and rocked once more.

As the sailor went back up the gangplank onto his ship, Drym climbed on to the front of the cart, took hold of the reins and set off for his home in the hamlet of Splatt.

He had decided to get the crate home before risking the first feeding.

FIFTY-EIGHT

Danglefang

Drym was thankful to have arrived home without incident.

The crate had been shifting and rocking all the way and he had been worried that the creature inside may actually break out.

Drym stopped in the lane by the side of his house and dropped down from the front of the cart.

His hands were trembling in a mixture of trepidation and excitement as he withdrew something wrapped in newspaper from his pocket. He unravelled the paper to reveal a large lump of red raw steak. It was dripping with blood.

'Mmmm, look at that, Spikey,' he said to his favourite sharp stick. 'Our new working pet is bound to like that, oh yes he is.'

Laying the steak on the ground a few paces in front of the crate door, Drym trembled again as he unlocked the padlock.

Then he pulled open the door, hiding behind it as he did so.

For a few seconds… nothing.

Drym peered around the side of the door.

Suddenly, a very strange creature scurried on all its eight legs out of the cage. The creature pounced on the steak as if it were live prey that had to be killed before it could be eaten.

Sqlch. Mnch. There were awful squelching and munching sounds as long canine fangs sank deep into the raw meat. Blood dripped on to the ground as a smirking Drym looked on in awe and whispered the creature's name under his breath…

'Danglefang.'

FIFTY-NINE

Working Wolfspider

Drym stared at his new working pet.

'Magnificent, oh yes he is,' he mumbled.

He couldn't take his eyes off the creature.

Danglefang was a wolfspider.

He had a mixed-up body, part wolf… and part spider.

He had eight hairy spider legs and wolf-like hair all over the rest of his body.

His head and jaw were mostly that of a wolf.

He had eight canine teeth – long fangs that protruded when he snarled.

But he had one spider trait that made him look especially scary… eight eyes.

Two eyes were wolf eyes, set roughly in the head where a wolf's would be.

His remaining six eyes were spider eyes.

The spider eyes were set around the back and sides of his head.

Drym now took a second piece of raw meat from his pocket and removed the newspaper from around it.

He then approached Danglefang cautiously, with the meat held out in one hand, but with his other hand holding Spikey in readiness to defend himself if necessary.

Drym dropped the second piece of meat.

The wolfspider immediately started devouring that too.

As yet more blood dripped on to the ground, Drym patted Danglefang on the head.

'Hello, boy. You're hungry, aren't you? Oh, yes you are.'

'Rrrrrrrrrrrrrrrrrr', the wolfspider growled a low growl.

It seemed he didn't like being patted.

Drym quickly stopped.

Dropping down yet another slab of raw meat on the ground, the nasty slaver read the paperwork that came with Danglefang, whilst the creature chomped and chewed on the meat.

The paperwork confirmed that the wolfspider was ideally suited to the task of catching children.

Firstly, his eight eyes gave him great all round vision.

And, with his eight long hairy legs, he could run very fast.

He was incredibly strong.

He could climb walls.

He could dangle upside down from ceilings.

He could squeeze into tight places.

He could set traps with his sticky web.

And, most important of all, when he caught up with fleeing or hiding children, he could inject a knockout poison with his fangs, then use his web to roll them in a cocoon and carry them back to his new master… Drym.

The creature would apparently respond well to training and tasks if rewarded at regular intervals with blood-soaked raw meat. Drym had been told that before delivery and it certainly seemed to be the case.

After reading all about the wolfspider for a second time, Drym congratulated himself. He was very pleased to have thought of ordering this new working mutant to help in his task of catching children and putting them in the slave dungeons.

With more lumps of raw steak, Drym led the creature to a large shed in the back garden that he had specially converted.

'There's your new kennel, Dang, boy,' he said, as he lobbed the meat in through the door.

'You get some rest and then, tomorrow, we'll begin our new job, oh yes we will.

'Together we'll be able to catch all the slavechildren we need.

'They won't stand a chance.

'Oh, no they won't!'

SIXTY

Five Hundred Slavechildren

Wendron was busy with her new job as Regulator of Schools.

She had also been busy setting up WENCO in Smogtown.

The wrinkled witch had worked out she would need at least five hundred slavechildren to work in the Skycycle and School Uniform factories, as well as the Wendroileum drilling fields. The two new dormitory buildings to accommodate the slave workers had just been finished.

So, Smogtown's WENCO was basically ready to go – both the factories and the fields – and Wendron was looking forward to starting production.

However… the witch had a pressing problem. She knew that Lister was having difficulty with the parents who were refusing to make *Lister's Choice*. They were simply not delivering their children to Drym and the Maggitts for selling as slaves.

This meant that there were no slaveworkers to launch WENCO and get Smogtown going.

So Wendron organised a meeting with Lister and travelled to his office in Nimdob to suggest a solution.

'All I want is five hundred slavechildren to work in my factories and fields,' she said to the Counterupper. 'I can round them up myself and you'll have five hundred names on your list in no time.'

SIXTY-ONE

A Standard Rate Per Child

Lister certainly liked the sound of getting a lot of names on his list quickly.

He knew Drym was on the case, but the Slaver-in-Chief hadn't yet reported any success.

The Counterupper was dreading his next meeting with King Manaccan when he'd have to tell him that the *Slavechildren* list was totally blank.

And what would the Emperor think of his failure when he arrived? Lister was very worried he may lose his job, or perhaps even his head.

Worse still, he may be sent to fight as a gladiator in the new Conquest Colosseum. That would be a horrible death.

So Lister was essentially very keen on Wendron's offer to get five hundred slavechildren on his list.

Although he did have one reservation.

'You do understand you'll still have to pay Mr Drym a fair fee under the slaving franchise contract,' he reminded the witch. 'And also the normal commission to *Maggitt & Maggitt*, the auctioneers.

'This will have to be the same fee and commission as they would have got if they'd collected and sold the children themselves.

'You see Miss Wendron, Drym and the Maggitts are responsible for gathering in the money paid for slaves and depositing it in the Royal Tax Coffers.

'The King and the Emperor would be very angry if they didn't get their share of the revenue.'

'Oh that's no problem at all,' said Wendron. 'I'll just be happy to get the workers so that Smogtown can get going. How about I pay a standard minimum rate? Shall we say… ten evos per child?

'Then Drym and the Maggitts can have their share and the King and the Emperor will get their taxes too. Everyone will be happy. It's a *Win-Win* deal.'

Lister was extremely content with that arrangement.

'That seals it then. I'll do the paperwork and make a copy of the list of the children from each family who could be taken as slaves, so you know which of them you are allowed to have.'

It was now official. Wendron had the necessary permission to round up five hundred slavechildren to work in her Smogtown factories and fields.

The wrinkled witch was ecstatic.

'We'll have our workers in no time,' she said to Scratchit as she made her way back from Lister's office to her Skycycle. 'And I'll soon have them working their little fingers to the bone for nothing but a dish of gruel and a crust of bread once a day.'

'Hssss.'

Scratchit hissed her appreciation as her mistress cackled manically.

'Hahahahahaaaa!'

SIXTY-TWO

Drym's Disappointment

Drym had been walking around in a fog of disappointment ever since learning that Wendron was going to collect five hundred children to work as slaves in her Smogtown factories and fields.

All the slavechildren collected by the witch were going to be paid for at a standard rate.

They were going to be assumed as worth only *ten* evos each.

And his commission – at the standard ten percent – would be just *one* evo per child.

'It's so unfair, Spikey,' he moaned, 'some of the children are worth far more than that, oh yes they are.'

But it wasn't just the money he was going to lose that was making him feel down.

He'd been *so* looking forward to rounding up the children and seeing the look on their faces when he lined them up and made *Lister's Choice*.

And he was especially looking forward to finding the frightened kids who were hiding, and sending Danglefang after those who made a run for it.

Now Wendron was going to spoil his fun as usual.

That would be five hundred families where *she* would have the enjoyment of making the choice and finding the hiders and chasing the runaways instead of him.

SIXTY-THREE

Find The Dog, Find The Diary

Drym scanned the copy of the list that Mr Lister had made for him. It detailed all the children who could be taken into slavery. He needed to see if there were any children he could collect quickly, before Wendron got to them.

From what he knew about them from the rubbish and other sources, there were some very special children, with various valuable talents, who would be worth a fortune at auction.

For example, from what he could remember from entries in his diary, a kid like Tommy Tremar, who could sing like an angel, would sell for perhaps *fifty* evos as a slavechild entertaining rich people at big houses and royal courts around the Empire. The franchise fee on these valuable children should be more like *five* evos, not just the one evo he would get under Wendron's system.

Thinking about all this suddenly made Drym realise something. Although a really valuable child like Tommy stuck in his memory, he couldn't remember *all* the details about *all* the other valuable children that he'd written in his diary.

It had taken him years to find out all the things he knew about the children. Not having the information was putting him at a disadvantage.

'We need our diary back, Spikey, oh yes we do.

'That little thief, Dribble, knows where it is, oh yes he does.

'If we can find the dog, we can find the diary.

'I wonder where the drooling little mutt could be?'

SIXTY-FOUR

We Know You're In There

The gnomes had first learned about *Edict Number II* from an article by Lester Lister in *The Daily Packet* newspaper.

Dribble listened as they discussed it in Seesaw's cottage.

'It says all gnomes and other sub-human species are to be enslaved with immediate effect,' said Swinger.

'*Sub-human species*!' complained Prickle. 'I'll give that Mr Lister a piece of my mind when I see him. I bet I can cook and clean and iron better than any human woman.'

'It's a good job we can read a bit,' said Plumper. 'Clevercloggs is always saying how important it is to learn as many words as we can. If we couldn't read, we wouldn't know about that new law.'

'Yes, but what should we *do*?' worried Greenfingers.

'I think we'll have to leave Washaway Wood as soon as possible,' said Swinger, 'before they come for us. We'll have to go and live in the forest or something.'

'But I can't leave my garden,' sighed Greenfingers. 'Who will care for my plants?'

'Oh, stop worrying about your silly shrubs,' scolded Prickle. 'Can't you see this is serious?'

Nck. Nck. Nck.

At that moment, there was a knock on the door.

'Who do you think it could be at this time of night?'

NCK! NCK! NCK!

'Open this door… we know you're in there.'

SIXTY-FIVE

The Kernish Soldiers Do Their Duty

Although his title was now "Commander-in-Chief" of the Kernish Army, General Warleggan's soldiers were all in Nimdob Gaol for refusing to carry out the order to enforce *Edict Number 1*. He therefore had no army to command.

The men had decided that, whatever the consequences, there was no way they were going to collect the children from their homes all around Kernowland and deliver them to the dungeons to be sold as slaves.

The good and loyal Kernish soldiers had, in the past, always done as they were told by their leaders and followed orders to the letter.

But, since Warleggan had taken charge, things had changed.

Even though they knew they would be severely punished – executed with the Guillotine of Sirap or sent to fight as gladiators in the new Conquest Colosseum – the order to collect slave-children went way beyond what they thought was their duty.

In fact, they had agreed unanimously, in a free and secret ballot, that it was their duty *not* to collect the children.

However, Manaccan had anticipated this reaction and arranged for the invader warlords in each of the eight new Regions of Wonrekland to send lots of their men to arrest the Kernish soldiers at gun- and sword-point in their beds.

SIXTY-SIX

Child-Seeking Slitherropes

With all his soldiers in gaol, Warleggan was waiting for a replacement army from outside Kernowland.

Manaccan had promised him that Empire soldiers were on their way who would be under his command and carry out his orders.

He was looking forward to that.

Meanwhile, he had quite a bit of spare time on his hands.

He had therefore jumped at the chance to help Wendron when he'd learned of her need for five hundred slavechildren to work in her Smogtown factory and fields.

'Of course, I'll help, Wendron, old dear,' he said when she asked him. 'It will be an absolute pleasure.'

As usual, where his favourite witch was concerned, Warleggan had been very thoughtful.

He had bred a batch of twenty-four of his beloved slitherropes.

But these were no ordinary slitherropes.

They were specially designed and trained to help Wendron capture the slavechildren she needed as fast as possible.

They were *child-seeking* slitherropes…

SIXTY-SEVEN

Nowhere To Run... Nowhere To Hide

Warleggan the warty warlock visited Coven Cave, taking the new batch of slitherropes with him in two of his Warcoat pockets.

Wendron greeted him with a freshly brewed cup of weed-leaf tea.

'Oh, you do make a lovely cup of weedy tea,' said Warleggan as he sipped it appreciatively.

'Hsssssssss!'

'Hsssssssss!'

'Hsssssssss!'

The ropes hissed and wriggled as he took them out to show her.

'Oh thank you, Warleggan,' said Wendron appreciatively.

'How thoughtful you are.

'Now we'll be able to find and catch the children much more quickly.'

'Yes, I'll say,' agreed Warleggan conspiratorially.

'Hahahahahaaaa!' cackled Wendron. 'When we chase the little brats with these special child-seeking slitherropes, they'll soon find they can't escape.

'There'll be nowhere to run... and nowhere to hide.'

SIXTY-EIGHT

Skycage v Gaol Cart

The race was on between Wendron and Drym to get the slavechildren rounded up.

Wendron had had help from Warleggan to construct a four-wheeled Skycage to attach to the back of her Skycycle.

The Skycage had folding black wings, just like the flying tricycle.

The wrinkled witch and the warty warlock had begun flying around Wonrekland collecting the children from the families identified by Lister's list.

Drym had heard about their early success and was resentful and demoralised. He knew his old cart – which was pulled slowly along the road by his scruffy old horse – was no match for Wendron's state-of-the-art airborne Skycage.

'It's not fair Spikey, oh no it isn't,' he said to the sharp stick. 'She's always spoiling our fun.

'*And* she's costing us lots of money with that standard rate deal she did with Lister.'

Drym then decided he just had to get on with it using the tools he had.

With lots of raw meat, he trained Danglefang to scuttle up and down the pile of rubbish at the back of his house rctrieving all the metal bars he could find.

Drym then bent the bars into shape before welding them to his cart to make a cage on the back.

He now had his own special gaol cart for collecting slavechildren

He was somewhat heartened as he admired the result.

'I suppose things aren't that bad, Spikey.

'That wretched witch may be able to fly around all over Wonrekland but we can still catch a few of the most valuable kids and transport them in our new gaol cart.

'We can only hope she'll soon have her five hundred slaveworkers rounded up, and then she won't bother us anymore, oh no she won't.'

SIXTY-NINE

Hunting For Slavechildren

Wendron had decided to start hunting for slavechildren in the town of Egdirbedaw.

It was just down the road from Splatt where Drym lived. She knew he was bound to find out what she was doing and took great delight in the thought that it would annoy her former pupil enormously.

She had despised all the children in her classes, but reserved a particular dislike for Drym.

She and Warleggan had decided that a good time for hunting children would be in the late afternoon – after school had finished, but before dinner time.

The children would normally be playing outside before they were called in to eat.

'Come along, Scratchit… and you too, Craw,' said Wendron as they set off.

'You can help with the hunt.'

SEVENTY

The Old Hagbag

As Drym was bumping along towards Towan Blystra in his rickety old gaol cart, he heard the familiar buzzing of the Skycycle engine overhead.

'Oh no, it's the old hagbag, Spikey,' he muttered. 'She can get around a lot quicker than we can in that flying machine of hers, oh yes she can. She's ruining our life again. But we'll get her back one day, oh yes we will.'

'Rrrrrrrrrrrrrrrrrr.'

Danglefang growled a low growl at the unfamiliar noise in the sky.

'No boy, you don't like the wrinkled old bully either, do you? Oh no you don't.'

Looking up to try to see Wendron in the sky, the former dustman soon spotted her.

He watched with a deepening frown as the flying trike – pulling the Skycage along behind it – headed for a town in the distance.

'She's hunting in Egdirbedaw,' he mumbled, in a voice that showed both his anger and his disappointment.

'She'll be able to steal a lot of *our* slavechildren from there.

'But at least it means she isn't going to get the kid we're after today, oh no she isn't.'

SEVENTY-ONE

Looking and Listening For Children

After circling above the town for a few minutes looking for somewhere to land the Skycycle and Skycage, Wendron finally chose a road on the outskirts.

Warleggan held on for dear life in his rear sidecar as they descended.

As usual, the landing wasn't a good one.

Wendron skidded off the road, mounted the kerb and narrowly missed running down a little old lady before smashing noisily into a garden wall.

After inspecting the Skycycle and Skycage and finding no significant damage, Wendron and Warleggan taxied down the road towards the centre of the town.

They were looking and listening for children under twelve.

Soon they could hear the sound of happy children laughing and shouting as they played in the next street.

The children were blissfully unaware of the danger that was lurking around the corner.

SEVENTY-TWO

Children At Play

'Children at play,' said Wendron, nastily. 'That's the sound we wanted to hear.'

'Indeed it is, Wendron old dear,' replied Warleggan.

The witch stopped the Skycycle and kept it idling just around the corner at the top of the street, taking care to ensure that none of the children could see them.

'Are you ready?'

'Totally,' came the reply as her companion in villainy first removed a dozen child-seeking slitherropes from a pocket on the right side of his Warcoat, and then another dozen from a pocket on the left.

'Hsssss.'

'Hsssss.'

'Hsssss.'

The slitherropes hissed and wriggled in his hands, as if they couldn't wait to be released to do their awful work.

SEVENTY-THREE

Seek Out Kids Who Try To Hide

'Now, do you remember the spellverse we decided on?' checked Wendron.

Wanting to take no chances, she had made up the verse herself so that the inept warlock knew exactly what he had to say.

'Surely do,' came the reply.

'Well then,' said the witch impatiently, 'get on with it, man.'

'Right you are,' said Warleggan, eager to please Wendron and also relishing the thought of the impending attack on the children. He then recited the agreed spellverse.

Seek out kids
Who try to hide
And drag them back here
By my side

With that, the grinning warlock released the hissing slitherropes.

'Hsssss.'

'Hsssss.'

'Hsssss.'

The ropes slithered off at great speed around the corner and hissed nastily as they snaked down the street… in the direction of the unsuspecting playing children.

SEVENTY-FOUR

'Hahahaaaaaaaaaaaa!' 'Charge!'

'Hahahaaaaaaaaaaaa!' screamed Wendron as she watched the slitherropes race away around the corner.

In the same moment, she quickly withdrew Whackit from her gown with her left hand whilst twisting back the throttle with her right.

Brrrmmmmmmmmmmm!

A puff of toxic black smoke belched from the back of the Skycycle as it roared into action.

'Hahahaaaaaaaaaaaa!'

'Charge!'

Witch and warlock cackled and yelled at the tops of their voices as they followed on behind the slitherropes into the street full of playing children.

Some were kicking a ball against a wall, others were skipping, two were playing hopscotch, four were playing a game of marbles.

'Crorrh!' Craw squawked as he flew off the handlebars into the air.

'Meeeowwwwwwwww!' mewed Scratchit in her meanest mew as she jumped from her basket.

The playing children all froze as they saw the slave hunters roaring towards them.

'HELLLLLPPPPPPP!'

'MUMMYYYYY!'

Then they screamed in fear and scattered in all directions.

SEVENTY-FIVE

Pandemonium

The terrified children ran through gates and down alleys to try to escape from their attackers. They jumped over walls and scrambled through hedges. But the slithering slitherropes spread out in all directions, each following a different child.

A hissing slitherrope wound around the ankle of one of the boys playing marbles. He fell over as he tried to kick it off with his other foot. He kept on kicking whilst on the ground but he couldn't release himself. The slitherrope began dragging him slowly back along the street towards the Skycage, tearing his shorts and grazing his legs as it did so.

There were yells and screams as the children were caught, one by screaming one, by the hissing ropes.

Now mothers joined in the pandemonium, running out of front doors armed with brooms and saucepans and rolling pins with which to protect their children.

'Get off of hi….'

Stnn!

'Leave her alo…!'

Stnn!

But Wendron was more than a match for them. She pointed Whackit at each mother in turn and stopped them in their tracks with a stunning spell.

The mothers dropped to the ground, defenceless against the powerful dark magic of the wrinkled witch.

SEVENTY-SIX

Truth Powder

The slitherropes dragged all the children back to the Skycage.

There were soon twenty-four of them gathered together by the side of it, all kicking and screaming and crying.

The stunnified mothers lay unconscious in the road and gardens.

'Give me the Truth Powder,' said Wendron to Warleggan.

Warleggan looked at the wrinkled witch admiringly.

He knew that, ever since they'd had trouble getting the gnomes to tell the truth, she'd been working on a powder to avoid that problem in the future. What a woman she is, he thought to himself.

The warlock drew a cylinder from his pocket and handed it over to the witch.

It had lots of holes in the end, a bit like a pepper pot.

Wendron held up the pot and Craw flew to her and took it in his claws.

He then flew into the air a few feet above the huddle of children and shook the pot, sprinkling them all with its contents as he did so.

'AHHHHHCHOOOOOOOOOO!'

All the children sneezed at once.

'Now, let's see if it works on a big group,' said Wendron.

'Children, I am Miss Wendron and I need to ask you some questions.

'Will you tell the truth?'

'*Yes, Miss Wendron,*' said all the children at once.

'Excellent,' said Wendron.
'Firstly, are you all aged twelve or under?'
'*Yes, Miss Wendron,*' said all the children.
'Excellent,' said Wendron.
'We can only take one child from each family.
'Hands up if you are the eldest or only child.'
Ten of the twenty-four children put their hands up.
'Hahahaaaaaaaaaaaa!' cackled Wendron triumphantly.
'Excellent!'

SEVENTY-SEVEN

A Skycage Full Of Slavechildren

'Get in the cage,' ordered Warleggan, to the ten eldest and only children who had put their hands up.

The ten did as they were told, each walking as if they were in some sort of trance.

The warlock was even more impressed with Wendron when he saw that the Truth Powder also seemed to make the children unusually obedient.

'Now, the rest of you, go home,' said Warleggan, pointing up the street as he did so.

The other children trudged away in the same trance-like manner as their friends and siblings.

How marvellous, children who do what they're told without question, thought the warlock as he watched them go.

'Well, get the door locked then, man,' instructed Wendron, when the ten slavechildren were sitting silently on the bench seats in the Skycage.

Warleggan was brought from his thoughts by Wendron's scolding.

He slammed the door, giving one last instruction as he turned the key in the lock.

'Seatbelts on.'

The children did as they were told whilst Warleggan jumped into his seat behind his favourite witch.

Wendron added Sparkit to the Wendroileum in the tank.

Putt, putt... brrrmmmmm.

A puff of smoke belched from the back of the Skycycle as it burst into life.

'Cfff.'

'Cfff.'

'Cfff.'

All the children coughed as the toxic black exhaust smoke filled the Skycage.

Wendron opened the throttle.

A jet of flame shot out of the trumpet exhaust.

'Eeeeeeeeeeeeeee.'

'Ahhhhhhhhhhhh.'

'Woahhhhhhhhhh.'

The trance induced by the Truth Powder had now worn off and all the children in the Skycage screamed with fear as the Skycycle pulled them along the street at breakneck speed.

'Hahahaaaaaaaaaaaa!'

As the Skycycle roared on down the street, Wendron looked behind and cackled manically above the noise of her flying contraption.

'Nothing beats a Skycage full of screaming slavechildren!'

Warleggan nodded in agreement... but his immediate concerns were actually elsewhere.

Surely the pilot should be looking forwards for take off!

The terrified warlock closed his eyes and gripped the sides of his seat as the Skycycle lifted off into the air... pulling the Skycage full of screaming children up behind it.

'EEEEEEEEEEEEEEEEEEE!'

'AHHHHHHHHHHHHHHH!'

'WOAHHHHHHHHHHHHH!'

'Excellent!' screeched Wendron at the top of her voice.

'Next stop... SMOGTOWN!'

SEVENTY-EIGHT

Working For WENCO

Smog Valley was on the horizon.

In the air, even from the relatively low height at which they were flying, the permanent murky mist that hung along its length was visible from miles away.

The ten slavechildren in the Skycage were silent, each wondering what would become of them and whether their families would miss them.

They descended through the cloud of smog and came out of it only a few feet from the ground. Wendron bounced down the valley runway, narrowly missing the row of mini hangars beside it before skidding into a muddy part of her back garden.

The children were marched, tied to each other by slitherropes, past one of the drilling fields and the Skycycle factory, before being lined up in front of the two dormitories that had been specially built to house them. Each had a sign above the door. One said, 'Girls', and the other said, 'Boys'.

Wendron now addressed the children as if they were in assembly at school.

'The Smogtown Skycycle and School Uniform factories, and the Wendroileum drilling fields, will be open 24 hours a day, and 7 days a week.

'You'll be working for WENCO in 20-hour shifts.

'Which means you'll get four hours to eat and sleep each day.

'And the rest of the time… you'll *WORK*!'

SEVENTY-NINE

Trouble At Tremar Farm

Half an hour after seeing Wendron in the sky heading towards Egdirbedaw, Drym arrived at Tremar Farm.

He was hunting for Tommy Tremar, the boy with the voice of an angel. Although Tommy was just six years old, Drym knew his value as a singing slave: at least fifty evos. Drym knew there were also two other children at the house who were under twelve. But Tommy's two twin sisters were just babies. Drym wanted the boy with the wonderful voice, not one of the babies… they'd be no use as slaves for years to come. He surveyed the house from all sides before giving Danglefang instructions and bribing him with a piece of raw meat. Then he knocked on the farmhouse door.

'I'm here on behalf of the King's Counterupper, to make *Lister's Choice*, oh yes I am. I've chosen your son, Tommy. He'll have to come with me. Oh yes he will.'

'Oh no he won't,' said Tommy's dad. With that, he knocked Drym to the ground and slammed the door.

But Danglefang had climbed silently into the house through an open window. He attacked Mr Tremar from behind, sinking his fangs deep into the defenceless man's flesh to knock him out before spinning him in a web cocoon, carrying him out of the house, and dumping him in the front yard.

Somewhat dazed, Drym got to his feet. Drawing Spikey from his belt, he swiped the sharp stick from side to side in rage…

Then he kicked open the door.

EIGHTY

'Leave My Children Alone'

Mrs Tremar had rushed downstairs to see what all the commotion was about. She came at Drym with a saucepan and hit him on the back of the head with it.

'Ouch! It hurts, oh yes it does,' yelled Drym, clutching his head where a large bump was forming.

Drym pushed the woman roughly to the ground. Then he took hold of her ankles and dragged her, screaming, with arms flailing, out of the front door and into the yard.

'Leave my children alone!'

'Now come on Mrs,' said Drym, 'you know I can take one of them, oh yes I can. It's the *LAW*! Oh yes it is.'

Outside, Danglefang wrapped a strand of his strong web around Mrs Tremar's ankle. Then he wrapped the other end around a thick gate post. She was now securely tied to the post.

Drym and Danglefang went inside once more and the nasty slaver locked the door behind him to block Tommy's escape.

Mrs Tremar screamed frantically from the gate post.

'Get out of my house! Leave my children alone.'

'Erherr!' 'Erherr!'

Drym and Danglefang searched around the farmhouse for little Tommy, accompanied all the while by the ever louder sound of the twins' crying.

'Someone help my babies!' screamed Mrs Tremar, even more frantically. 'Pleassse, help my babies!'

EIGHTY-ONE

A Place A Boy Would Hide

'Erherr!'

'Erherr!'

Drym ignored Tommy's mum's frantic pleas as he and his wolfspider carried on hunting for the little boy.

They pulled open cupboards and pushed over wardrobes.

'Erherr!'

'Erherr!'

The babies cried and cried and cried.

Upstairs, on the landing, Danglefang ran up the wall, raced across the ceiling, and pushed open the loft hatch.

'Erherr!'

'Erherr!'

The hairy hunter entered the loft and searched it thoroughly.

When he emerged in the hatch again, without their prey, Drym spoke his thoughts aloud.

'Where could he be, Dang?'

As he said this, the nasty grey man was looking out of the upstairs window and across the yard.

Then he saw it.

The barn.

'Ahhhaahhhhhhhhh!

'Now there's a place a boy would hide…

'Oh yes it is.'

EIGHTY-TWO

Tommy's Special Hiding Place

Tommy Tremar, who had only just survived his encounter with the hungry trogs, was in his special hiding place. He hid there sometimes when he'd been naughty and dad was cross with him. His hiding place was in the barn. It was in a big wooden box behind the cow milking pens.

Some of the farm equipment was kept in the box. But Tommy had discovered – when he was five – that he could fit in the box with the equipment… and close the lid.

And nobody knew he was in there.

There were even some holes in the box that he could peer out of. The holes also made sure he could breathe when he was in there.

Tommy had heard his mum and dad talking one evening about *Lister's Choice*. They had not been able to make the decision to send one of their children into slavery but knew that, when the slavers came looking, they'd probably take Tommy as he was the only child in the Tremar family who could work. The babies were far too young.

Tommy had decided there and then that he would hide in his special hiding place if the slavers ever came to his house.

Drym entered the barn, with Danglefang following closely behind him.

Tommy was already shivering with fear inside his hiding box. But he began to tremble uncontrollably when he saw the hairy, scary, mutant creature that had come in with Drym.

EIGHTY-THREE

I Smell A Boy Child

Snff. Snff.

Drym sniffed the air.

'I smell a boy child. We need to find it. I'll check this end, you take that end.'

Danglefang had quickly learned he'd get plenty of lovely raw meat if he did what his new master wanted.

So he was more than happy to comply with instructions.

He knew that the sooner he got the job done, the sooner he would get fed.

Tommy was still watching through the hole in the box.

As Drym climbed the wooden ladder into the loft, the little lad was amazed to see the wolfspider fire a long strand of webbing at a roof girder above the box.

The web strand stuck fast as soon as it made contact with the wooden beam.

Then Tommy saw something even more amazing.

The wolfspider shot through the air along the strand of webbing, which retracted into his body as he flew.

'What a hunter, eh Spikey?' said Drym, as he admired Danglefang's web-assisted jump.

'Much more fun than that dozy, drooling dog.'

Clnk.

There was an awful clunk as Danglefang landed on top of Tommy's hiding place.

EIGHTY-FOUR

A Horrible Scratching

'Rrrrrrrrrrrrrrrrrr.' Scrtch. Scrtch. Scrtch.

'Rrrrrrrrrrrrrrrrrr.' Scrtch. Scrtch. Scrtch.

There was a horrible scratching sound on top of the box as the wolfspider growled and tried to open the lid with his legs.

'You've found him straight away,' yelled Drym in almost demented excitement. 'Well done, Dang!'

Tommy grabbed hold of a strap and held the lid down as best he could from inside the box.

One of the creature's hairy feet came in through the hole that Tommy had been peering through. Tommy recoiled and gripped harder on the strap. Then another foot came in through another hole. Tommy gripped harder still. But the lid began to open. The little boy was no match for the wolfspider's strength.

'Hellllllpppppppppp!!!' screamed Tommy, no longer able to contain his fear.

But there was nobody to help him. Dad was still cocooned.

Mum screamed and screamed: 'Leave my children alone! HELLLPP! Somebody… please help us!'

But she was still web-tied to the gate post.

'RRRRRRRRRRRRRRRRRRRRR!'

Danglefang growled even more ferociously as he pulled open the lid of the box with one concerted effort.

Tommy looked up. A horrible, smirking, grey face was looking down into the box. 'Bring him, Dang!'

EIGHTY-FIVE

Eight More Slavechildren

Tommy Tremar looked around at the other children in Drym's gaol cart as it wound slowly along the lanes towards Polperro.

After catching Tommy at Tremar Farm and throwing him in the cage, Drym had stopped at a dozen or so houses on the way.

At eight of the houses, there was a child of twelve or under who was eligible to be included in the *Slavechildren* list.

None of the parents was prepared to make *Lister's Choice*.

So Drym – with Danglefang's help – had been very happy to make it for them.

There had been more fighting and pleading and screaming. But the wolfspider was too strong for any of the parents, and he and Drym had won the fight every time.

Tommy felt as sorry for all the other eight children in the gaol cart as he felt for himself.

But most of the time, he couldn't stop thinking and worrying about his mum and dad, and his baby sisters.

As Drym had taken Tommy away in the cart, he'd seen his dad bound in the web cocoon and his mum tied to the gatepost. And he'd heard his little sisters still screaming inside the house.

Tommy knew that Mrs Saltash from the village would be visiting that afternoon to deliver the new curtains. He hoped and hoped that she would come as soon as possible and release his parents so they could look after the twins.

EIGHTY-SIX

'Jump In There!'

When they got to the town, Drym's gaol cart made its way around the back of the Polperro Inn, along the track that the Maggitts had made especially for the purpose.

Drym jumped down from the cart and opened the iron door in the wall of the inn, revealing the entrance to the slave chute.

Then he opened the door at the back of the gaol cart.

'Dang! In!'

Danglefang jumped into the cart.

'Rrrrrrrrrrrrrrrrrrrrr.'

All the children recoiled and pushed themselves back against the bars as the wolfspider growled and snarled menacingly at them.

With Danglefang guarding the open cage door, Drym backed the cart right up against the entrance to the slave chute.

Danglefang now moved down one side of the cart towards the back, forcing all the children down the other side... towards the cage door and the slavechute entrance.

Tommy was now furthest from the cage door.

He would be last out.

Drym pointed at the chute entrance and shouted at the child nearest the door.

'Jump in there!'

EIGHTY-SEVEN

'Make Her, Dang'

'Jump in there!'

The child nearest the gaol cart door was a girl called Rebecca, or Becky for short.

Despite Drym's repeated order to jump, she didn't move at all. Tommy could see she was very scared of jumping into the chute.

'Make her, Dang,' said Drym.

'Rrrrrrrrrrrrrrrrrrrr.'

With that, the wolfspider growled again as he started moving slowly towards the terrified young girl.

That did it for Becky. Whatever was down that chute couldn't possibly be as scary as the eight-eyed, eight-legged, fang-toothed, hairy wolfspider that was growling towards her in the cart. The little girl jumped into the open chute.

'EEEEeeeeeeeeeeeeeeeeeeeeeeeeeeeeeeeeeee!'

The other children heard her scream fade as she slid down the slide.

A trembling Tommy watched as all the other children were made to jump into the chute.

'Rrrrrrrrrrrrrrrrrrrr.'

Danglefang was now snarling and growling at Tommy as the terrified boy looked at the entrance to the chute.

There was no escaping it. It was his turn next.

He had to do it.

He jumped.

EIGHTY-EIGHT

The Crowded Dungeon

Tommy slid down the slide inside the slave chute.

He got to the bottom and shot out of the other end very fast, landing on the child who had jumped in before him.

Drym had been busy.

The darkened dungeon was already overcrowded.

The new arrivals began chattering.

'Sqrrrrr!'

Ratchet squeakgrowled through the bars at the newly arrived children.

'Shhhhhhh. They don't like us talking,' said a voice from the corner.

'Sqrrrrr!'

'Sqrrrrr!'

Two more rattweilers were now staring through the bars at the children. One had climbed the torch holder and another sat on the dungeoneer's stool.

All the new arrivals became quiet as the rattweilers stared into the cell.

Tommy glanced at their infra-red eyes. They all seemed to be staring at *him*. He looked away quickly, down at the floor, hoping they hadn't taken exception to him glancing at them.

Apparently content that they'd made their point, the rattweilers padded away down the dark, dingy corridor.

It was now that Tommy became conscious of the noise made by the moleworms as they dug out the other dungeons.

EIGHTY-NINE

The Opatseg

Superintendent Scurvy was thoroughly enjoying his new role as Chief of Police.

The thousand rogues he had brought in from all over the Empire were now installed and operating as a secret police force. They were doing their job of spying on the people very well, creating an atmosphere of uncertainty and suspicion.

The secret police force was feared all over Erthwurld.

They controlled the people using Terror.

They were known as… *The Opatseg*.

It was Scurvy's job, through the Opatseg, to make sure that the lives of the people of Wonrekland were filled with an ever-present fear of Evile.

In accordance with *Edict Number VIII*, the Emperor's emblems, edifices, and effigies were going up all over the newly conquered territory. Flags, busts, statues, pictures, murals, mosaics… Evile was everywhere.

Evstika banners were draped on public buildings, and every house had to have an Evstika flag flying from it, whether the owner liked it or not. If people objected, Scurvy confiscated their homes and gave them to his henchmen.

He had already confiscated the homes of all the people on his *Rebels and Troublemakers* list, and handed the properties over to members of the Opatseg.

The reign of Terror in Wonrekland had well and truly begun.

NINETY

Half An Onion And Raw Cabbage

Louis was now barely able to stay conscious. He was very weak from lack of food. Although the prisoner was only allowed a few mouldy biscuits and water once a day, Purgy was stealing and eating some of his rations. Even the food he did get was so horrible it made him ill. He had vomited three or four times a day for more days than he could remember. One morning, Purgy himself was sick from eating Louis' food.

Jenny had learned that Louis was Tizzie's brother. She suggested to the tattooed pirate that she went down into the hold with Louis' rations. Purgy agreed.

Down in the hold, Jenny spoke to the sickly young boy in her warm, kind voice: 'I've been hearing you being sick. You must eat something. I got you this.' With that, she held out half an onion and a piece of raw cabbage. 'Sorry they're not cooked but you need to eat, and this is all I could get from the galley.'

'Thanks,' said Louis weakly. The pirates had been so mean. It was a great comfort that someone was being nice to him. He was so hungry, he began chewing the onion and cabbage straight away. Whilst Louis ate, Jenny bathed the raw skin around his wrists and ankles where the shackles were rubbing constantly and making his skin bleed.

'I'll try to bring you some more food if I get the chance.'

'Thanks,' said Louis again, before drifting off into his hunger-induced sleep once more.

NINETY-ONE

The New Wurld

As Bella's ship, *HMS Kernowland*, sailed into Ekaepasehc Bay, she listened carefully as the first officer briefed his crew on the history of the area.

'Long ago, a few people from Eporue travelled west in tiny wooden ships and landed in this very same part of Acirema North.

'These early explorers entered this huge bay, before sailing deeper into the continent along the River Natahwop. Some way up the river, they established a little fortified town on an island. This first settler town was named, "Enwotsemaj".

'The continent was previously unknown to anyone in the Empire, so it was soon being referred to by these first settlers as, the "New Wurld".

'But there were already people living there, the Native Aciremans, who called themselves, "Redskins".

'The settlers soon began trading with the Redskins, and Acirema North grew ever more prosperous as wave upon wave of people came here from all over Erthwurld, to escape Evile's tyranny and take part in the building of the New Wurld.

'The tribes of Acirema North are strong and numerous,' concluded the first officer. 'They and the settlers have been resisting Evile for a long time. We hope the people here will agree to help us to repair our ships and regroup, so that one day we can launch a counter attack to free Kernowland.

'We've asked for a meeting with Chief Natahwop.'

NINETY-TWO

Kroy Wen City

Kroy Wen City came into view as *The Kernow Queen* made for the harbour at the mouth of the Nosduh River.

The city had been built by settlers from all over Erthwurld, many of whom had followed the original Enwotsemaj settlers and come to escape the Empire and build new lives in the vast New Wurld.

The settlers in this part of Acirema North had decided that the eastern end of Gnol Island, in the estuary of the Nosduh River, was a good place to build a city.

In a short time, they had established five distinct city areas, which they called 'boroughs': Nattahnam, Nylkoorb, Sneeuq, Xnorb, and Netats Island.

Nattahnam was the most populated and built-up place.

As the merchant ship entered Kroy Wen harbour, those sailors on board who hadn't been there before looked at the shoreline in disbelief.

Cule couldn't believe his eyes either as he viewed Nattahnam from the deck of the ship.

NINETY-THREE

The Secret Rendezvous

HMS Kernowland had finally sailed through Ekaepasehc Bay and entered the Natahwop River, just as the day's light was fading.

'We'll drop anchor here and get drinking water for the trip up river to Enwotsemaj,' said Admiral Crumplehorn. After the water had been collected, the ship sailed west along the river, travelling deeper and deeper into Acirema North.

Bella lost count of the number of wharfs along the banks of the river.

'What are they all for?' she asked one of the older officers.

'Tobacco is grown in this region,' came the reply. 'They put it in huge barrels for storage. Each wharf serves a plantation. Ships dock at the wharfs and transport the barrels down to the bay, where they are sent all around the wurld.'

When the Guardians of Kernow arrived at Enwotsemaj, they learned that a message had been sent by Chief Natahwop.

The Admiral and his officers could rendezvous with the leader of the Redskins at a secret location in the forest.

Two of the chief's most trusted and loyal braves would act as guides.

Bella was most honoured to learn that, although only a lieutenant, she would be attending the meeting because she was the highest ranking dolphineer in the company.

She was so excited that she would soon meet the legendary Redskin chief.

NINETY-FOUR

Cloudscrapers

As Cule stared in wonder at Nattahnam, he heard the appreciative comments of those other men on the boat who, like him, had never been to Kroy Wen before.

'Wow, cloudscrapers.'

'They say they're the tallest buildings in the wurld.'

'Look at that one, it must be higher than a mountain!'

The cloudscrapers were truly magnificent.

The young Kernish warrior had heard about these 'tall buildings that nearly reach the clouds', but no amount of hearing about them could have prepared him for actually seeing them.

Cule had also heard that Xnorb Zoo had some very strange animals from all over Erthwurld in it, and was hoping he might get the chance to go there.

'Make ready for port!'

Cule was brought from his thoughts by the Captain's order to dock the vessel.

He now concentrated on the reason he was here: to meet other rebels and join the fight against the Empire.

He had memorised his instructions, and knew he had to find his way to a boarding establishment called, *The Blarney House*.

After docking, Cule threw his sailor's rucksack over his shoulder and disembarked.

He headed for Nylkoorb.

NINETY-FIVE

The Blarney House

Cule arrived in Nylkoorb just before dark.

He asked for directions from five people, and gradually got nearer to his destination with the information he received from each person he spoke to.

When he finally arrived at *The Blarney House* it was late in the evening. He first made sure he'd remembered the secret message to identify himself. He also made sure he went around to the back of the house as he had been told to do.

Then he took a deep breath and knocked on the door.

He heard heavy footsteps and a creak as the thick wooden door opened.

A huge man with curly red hair now filled the doorway.

'Whaddyawant at me back door at this time of night, young fella!?'

Cule took a step backwards, somewhat surprised by the man's gruff manner and massive frame.

Recovering quickly, he said the secret message.

'I am a hungry sailor from over the sea. I need a friendly place to stay before I go home.'

'I was once the same, though I never went home. But one day I will,' came the reply.

Cule sighed.

He was very relieved.

He now knew he was talking to a fellow rebel.

NINETY-SIX

Brendan Blarney

'Brendan Blarney! At your service, lad,' said the man as he held out his hand in greeting.

Cule took hold of the shovel-like hand that was offered to him.

Brendan Blarney squeezed hard. Cule squeezed back. He had won the junior arm wrestling championship of Kernowland for the last three years, so he was very, very strong.

But the young man quickly realised he had met more than his match... Blarney was a muscle monster!

'Come in quickly, and get we'll get some stew inside you.'

The red-haired monster pulled Cule forward as he spoke.

Cule was dragged into the kitchen of the house.

Inside it was warm and cosy. A log fire burned in the hearth. A big pot bubbled above the fire.

'Me daughter's upstairs. She'll be down shortly. Then we'll eat.'

Cule glanced at the bubbling pot and suddenly realised how hungry he was. He hadn't eaten since breakfast.

Blarney noticed his guest looking longingly at the stew.

He immediately strode over to the back of the kitchen, opened a narrow door and shouted up the stairs that were behind it.

'EMILYYYYYY!'

Cule heard footsteps hurrying across the ceiling.

The footsteps then started down the stairs.

NINETY-SEVEN

Emily

A teenage girl came into the kitchen smiling. Cule guessed her age at about fourteen.

'This is me daughter, Emily. We can speak freely around her. She's as much a rebel fighter as you or me, lad. More so, some would say.'

'Glad to hear it,' said Cule, smiling at Emily. 'We need all the help we can get if we're going to defeat the Empire.'

Emily pushed her red hair away from her face and smiled back, as her father replied.

'One step at a time, young fella! Co-ordinated action all over Erthwurld. Teamwork. That's what'll get rid of the Emperor.'

'Yes, of course,' agreed Cule. 'That's why I'm here. To join others who are resisting the Emperor's evil and tyranny.'

Emily now spoke as she dished out the stew: 'So you're the famous trog fighter… I thought you'd be bigger.'

'Emily,' frowned Blarney senior, 'remember he's a guest.'

'Just joking,' smiled Emily. 'So… were you scared?'

'Very…' said Cule. 'But they ate my gran and would have done the same to all the other old people in the town. I had to stop them.' The mood in the kitchen suddenly became more serious and sombre. Emily seemed unsure as to what to say.

'You did what you had to do, lad,' said her father. 'And we're very glad to have such a brave young warrior here with us. We've arranged for you to meet the others tomorrow.'

NINETY-EIGHT

The Rebels Of Acirema North

Next morning, Cule was awoken very early by Mr Blarney.

After a hearty breakfast, he and the two Blarneys travelled on a ferry boat to Netats Island.

Once on the island, they walked a long way until they came to the edge of a huge expanse of trees.

'Tlebneerg Forest,' said Emily. 'Only another couple of hours and we'll be there.'

Three hours later, they came to a large open expanse of grassland within the forest.

A big, single storey, log building had been built where the forest met the grassland.

Just in front of the building, there was a square of about fifty paces long on each side, where the grass had been cut very short.

'Why do they cut the grass?' asked Cule.

'That's the Landing Square,' replied Emily, as if he should have known it.

Mr Blarney gave five distinct knocks on the door.

Cule guessed this was probably a secret means of identifying visitors as friends.

The door opened and the trio went inside.

NINETY-NINE

Unfair Taxes

Throughout the day in the log cabin, Cule was introduced to many other members of RAE, who seemed to be arriving from all over the northeastern part of Acirema North to this remote place in the forest.

He also learned more details from Mr Blarney about the history of this land, and why so many of the settlers were rebelling against Evile.

Evile had not taken much notice of the settlers at first.

But then the great continent began to do very well and produced lots of goods and services and sold them all over Erthwurld for big profits.

Evile then took an interest.

He wanted his tax revenues.

But, for some reason, perhaps because the New Wurld was doing so well, the Emperor made the taxes twice as much as they were anywhere else in Erthwurld.

The settlers of Acirema North were not at all happy to pay such unfair taxes, especially since they had no say in what the money would be spent on.

So Evile sent in his ships and troops to take control of the eastern states.

In a very short time, he had imposed Imperial Martial Law.

ONE HUNDRED

Imperial Tax Inspectors

Imperial Tax Inspectors made sure everyone in Acirema North paid the Emperor's tax demands.

The unfair taxes created great hardship for the settlers, and stifled the growth of the New Wurld.

And, to make matters much worse, in their position of unbridled power, Evile's cronies behaved very badly.

They regularly confiscated the land and goods of those who couldn't pay their taxes, using force to take things for themselves and their family and friends.

Most settlers had come to Acirema North to get as far away from the Empire and its ways as possible.

But now the Empire had followed them with a vengeance.

Having learned all about the history of Acirema North, Cule could understand why the settlers had been joining the resistance in their thousands.

ONE HUNDRED & ONE

Chief Natahwop

The Guardians of Kernow were met at Enwotsemaj by the Redskin guides who had been sent, as promised, by Chief Natahwop.

They were then led north into a forest by their guides.

After about half-a-day's walk, they arrived at the secret meeting point.

It was a large clearing in the forest.

When they arrived, Bella was enthralled by what she saw.

There were at least fifty Redskins sitting in a big circle.

Chief Natahwop looked very impressive in his colourful clothes and headdress of feathers.

On the chief's left sat an older woman, of about his own age, whom Bella assumed was his wife.

On his right was a beautiful young woman of about Bella's own age.

ONE HUNDRED & TWO

Great Waterfall And *Playful One*

The meeting in the forest began with Chief Natahwop explaining what had happened when Evile had invaded ten years previously.

The Emperor had taken the chief's wife hostage and threatened to take his eight-year-old daughter and all the other Redskin children into slavery.

This is when he had decided that, for her own safety, little Princess Satnohacop should escape to Kernowland, the only place in Erthwurld where the Emperor's tentacles had not yet penetrated.

However, as a punishment for his daughter's escape, the chief was humiliated by Evile.

Not only were place names in his land turned backwards, but he had to turn his own name backwards too.

Natahwop agreed to all the humiliations in order to protect his people from Evile's wrath, especially the children.

Bella now learned that the chief's real name was, *Powhatan*, which meant *Great Waterfall* in his own language.

In the same way, his daughter was really called, *Pocahontas*, which meant *Playful One* in her own language.

At this point in his retelling of events, the proud Redskin chief paused, as if he were about to say something important…

'But the time has come to begin the rebellion. We will no longer submit to Evile's tyranny. From this moment on, we will be using our birth names as they were given to us.'

ONE HUNDRED & THREE

The Clevernote

Chief Powhatan went on to describe to Admiral Crumplehorn how his resolve had been bolstered when he received a note from Clevercloggs the Explorer.

After ten years in hiding, his daughter had risked great danger by breaking her cover and returning from Kernowland to deliver it to him.

He was so glad to see her again.

She had grown into a beautiful, courageous, and independent young woman, and he was so very proud of her.

'The note was a Clevernote,' said Powhatan.

'Ah, communications in the invisible writing invented by Clevercloggs?' said the Admiral, nodding to show that he knew all about them.

'Yes,' said the chief, 'so there would be no evidence if Pocahontas had been captured on her way home to us.'

'Very sensible,' said the Admiral...

'And what did the Clevernote say?'

ONE HUNDRED & FOUR

'We'll Be Flying'

'Clevercloggs said that, with the fall of Kernowland, the time had come for all the good people of Erthwurld to rise up and fight back against Evile and his Empire of Evil,' said Chief Powhatan.

'If I agreed that the time was right, Clevercloggs asked me to arrange for a Great Powwow to take place at Tipi City in Prairieland. 'He suggested we invite the leaders of the rebel settlers as well, as they would be good allies in the battle against Evile.

'Very sound thinking,' nodded the Admiral.

'We thought so, too,' said Powhatan. 'The Great Powwow has been convened. It will take place in Tipi City, and the leaders of all the tribes and settlers from all over Acirema North are going to be there.

'All the tribes?' queried Admiral Crumplehorn, 'that's some consensus.'

'Yes,' agreed the chief. 'It was when the chiefs learned that Clevercloggs the Explorer had called the meeting, and would speak there, that they all agreed to attend. Everybody in Erthwurld knows that, when the wise old gnome speaks, it is a good idea to listen.'

'But it's a long way to Tipi City,' said the Admiral. 'It will take us many days to get there on horseback.'

'I know,' answered Chief Powhatan...

'That's why we'll be flying.'

ONE HUNDRED & FIVE

'Here Comes Your Ride'

By mid-afternoon, it seemed that everyone who was going to arrive at the big log cabin in the clearing in the forest on Netats Island, had done so.

As evening drew in, Mr Blarney, Cule, and Emily went outside to stand on the front porch.

'What are we waiting for?' asked Cule.

'Oh, I forgot to tell you,' said Mr Blarney. 'Emily and I have to go back home....'

He paused before continuing.

'But we've arranged for you to go with some of the others here to the Great Powwow in Tipi City.'

Before Cule could ask anything about powwows and tipis, Emily pointed to the sky.

'Look!

'Here comes your ride now.'

ONE HUNDRED & SIX

Bounty Money

The Revenger had made very good time on its way back to Wonrekland.

A message bird had been sent ahead to say that they had Prince Louis on board, with an offer of an exchange of the wanted assassin for the bounty money.

Despite assurances he had received to the contrary, Captain Pigleg would not agree to enter a port for fear of arrest. He was wanted for piracy in so many places that he did not feel it wise to dock in any place where they knew he was coming in advance.

Instead it had been arranged that Superintendent Scurvy would sail out two kiloms from shore on a small navy vessel, which would meet *The Revenger* in open water.

There the handover of the prisoner would take place.

The pirates would be given the bounty.

The boy prince would be taken back to shore.

Pigleg could sail away.

Scurvy was coming in person because he wanted to check the identity of the prisoner. Having seen Louis before, he was confident he could remember what he looked like.

Flying the new Royal Flag of Wonrekland – a big red 'M' for 'Manaccan' on a black background – the navy boat came alongside *The Revenger*.

Down in the hold, Louis wondered what all the commotion up on deck was about as Scurvy boarded the pirate ship.

ONE HUNDRED & SEVEN

I Need To See The Prisoner

'Mr Scurvy, greetings, so good to see you again,' said Mr Cudgel.

'*Superintendent* Scurvy, if you don't mind,' said the Chief of Police, with the snarl he reserved for anyone who showed a lack of respect for his new position.

A trickle of blood ran down his chin as he continued: 'Shall we get straight to business?'

Click, thud. Click, thud. Click, thud.

Pigleg paced forward across the deck.

'That's what we're here for... *Superintendent.*'

Scurvy's snarl turned into a crooked smile.

'Captain, as you can see, down there on that vessel we have a large money chest.'

'It seems that you have,' said Pigleg, peering over the side rail. 'So why don't we just haul it on board as agreed.'

'Well, Captain, I'm sure you'll agree that before I part with it, I need to see the prisoner. Just to confirm his identity, you understand.'

'That's fair enough,' agreed Pigleg. 'Mr Cudgel, make it so.'

Cudgel nodded to Purgy.

The tattooed pirate descended into the hold with three other heavily armed men. He was taking no chances with that dangerous assassin down there.

ONE HUNDRED & EIGHT

A Bag Of Bones

'Right, prisoner boy, get up on deck, now,' ordered Purgy as he warily released Louis from his shackles whilst the other pirates pointed their muskets at him.

Louis climbed the steps and emerged a few moments later, looking very much the worse for his voyage in the hold.

Although naturally a very slight lad, without an inch of fat on his whole body, Louis had still lost a lot of weight on the journey. He was little more than a bag of bones. But hc was still recognisable as the boy Scurvy had first seen at the Polperro Inn.

'So… we meet again,' said the Superintendent. 'Spellcaster! Thief! Assassin! You'll be punished for all your crimes now.'

'The lad looks a teeny, tiny bit small to be all those bad things in such a little parcel, don't ye think mates?' roared Pigleg.

'Aye, Cap'n,' roared his men in unison.

'Don't you be so sure, Captain Pigleg,' said Scurvy. 'Boy or not, he's a vicious, murdering little thug: a real villain through and through.'

'Well, if he's as bad as you say, I'm sure he'll get what's coming to him,' said Pigleg, as he pushed Louis forward into the clutches of Wonrekland's Chief of Police.

'Yes, he's going to stand trial and then he'll be for the chop. But not until I've had his teeth to replace the ones I've got that are falling out. And not until he's given me back my key.'

ONE HUNDRED & NINE

'Did You Say… *Key*?'

'Did you say… *key*?'

'I did indeed, Captain. Amongst his many other crimes, the boy's a key thief.'

'Well, well, well,' said Pigleg, unable to believe his luck at encountering such a bad barterer as Scurvy undoubtedly was. The Chief of Police had already shown far too much interest in the key, so giving away to Pigleg that it was very valuable.

'I believe we have your key, Superintendent,' said the Captain, 'but we'll need to haggle over the price.'

'I am… er… authorised to… er… give you... er... 100 evos for all his possessions,' stuttered Scurvy.

He clearly wasn't used to bartering.

Pigleg, on the other hand, was. He slowly opened the little chest containing all Louis' possessions.

The Golden Key sat on top.

Pigleg picked it up and slowly held it out so that it was just inches from Scurvy's nose.

The Chief of Police could barely contain his excitement.

His glee at the chance of recovering the key he had lost was obvious to his bartering adversary.

Pigleg read all the signs and set his price.

'1,000 evos…'

Scurvy made no further attempt to haggle.

'Done.'

ONE HUNDRED & TEN

Bring The Prisoner

Having identified that Louis was indeed the fugitive they were seeking, and negotiated for the little chest containing the boy's possessions, including the Golden Key, Scurvy gave instructions and four of his men helped the pirates haul a large chest onto *The Revenger.*

Pigleg pulled open the chest with his hook.

'There are 6,000 gold evo coins in there, Captain,' said Scurvy. '5,000 for the assassin, and 1,000 for his possessions as agreed. Would you like to count it?'

'No I don't think so,' said Pigleg. 'After all, if we can't trust a King, who can we trust?'

'Very well,' said Scurvy as yet another trickle of blood oozed down his chin and dripped on to the deck. 'Then I'll be getting along.'

Scurvy then gave the order to his men.

'Bring the prisoner. And watch him. He's dangerous.'

With that, the shackles were put back on Louis and he was lowered onto the navy boat.

His clothes had been torn on his adventures, and his Kernow Cape and uniform jacket had been lost in Jungleland.

So, what with all that had happened to him, and his near starvation on his most recent journey, it was a very scrawny and untidy looking boy who was put on to the navy vessel for transporting back to shore.

ONE HUNDRED & ELEVEN

Tummy Ache

Once in port, Louis was pushed along the dock very roughly by a couple of soldiers.

They really seemed to have it in for him.

He could hardly walk and his tummy ached constantly.

At the end of the dock, he was thrown into a gaol wagon, ready for transporting to Kernow Castle.

A guard chucked a scrap of bread in through the bars of the cage. Louis grabbed up the bread and gulped it down.

But he was *so* very thirsty.

What he really wanted was water.

Another guard put a tankard filled with water through the bars.

Louis went to take it, but the guard suddenly tipped the tankard forward and threw its contents in Louis' face.

'My brother was one of the guards you killed,' said the man angrily, before he was pulled away by an officer who spoke in a raised voice.

'There'll be no maltreatment of prisoners on my watch, Corporal Porkellis. It's our job to get him to the castle where the proper authorities can deal with him. And then, when he's been tried and sentenced, you can go to the execution.'

Louis knew that didn't sound good for him.

But he was now so weak with hunger and thirst that he just lay on the floor of the gaol wagon and went to sleep.

ONE HUNDRED & TWELVE

A Very Close Shave

Mr Scurvy hurried ahead of the gaol wagon transporting Louis to the castle.

He couldn't wait to show his King the little chest of treasure containing Louis's things that he'd got from Pigleg for only 1,000 evos.

Most importantly, he wanted to hand over the Golden Key that he thought Louis had stolen at the Polperro Inn.

Scurvy thought he'd just about got away with blaming the loss on Louis, by saying he'd stolen it.

But the key had been one of the main things Manaccan had wanted to present as a gift to the Emperor on his arrival.

So the King had not been at all pleased at the loss, and Scurvy was sure he'd gone down in his leader's estimation after that.

Now was his chance to make amends.

On arrival at the castle, Scurvy sent a message to the King and was granted an immediate audience.

'Well done, Scurvy. I always knew I could rely on you,' lied Manaccan.

'Oh, thank you, your Majesticness,' snivelled Scurvy. 'I do try my best to please.'

'I'll lock this in the cabinet in the Map Room personally,' said the King. 'The Emperor need never know it was gone.'

Phew, all's well that ends well, I suppose, thought Scurvy as he left. But that was a very close shave.

ONE HUNDRED & THIRTEEN

Scurvy's Prisoner Problem

Still basking in the praise he received from King Manaccan for the capture of Prince Louis and the recovery of the lost Golden Key, Sheviok Scurvy was very pleased with himself.

However, in one area of his activities, Scurvy was a victim of his own success...

And that very success was in danger of undermining his other recent achievements.

He had done such a good job identifying and arresting all the people on the *Rebels and Troublemakers* list that Nimdob Gaol had found it hard to accommodate them all.

Then, with the arrest of all the teachers that Wendron had recommended for execution, and all the soldiers that had refused to obey the order to enforce *Edict Number 1*, and all the gnomes, and everyone else, the gaol had become full to overflowing.

Scurvy's success in arresting people and charging them with all sorts of unfounded accusations had actually created a prisoner problem.

There were so many prisoners, it was standing room only at the gaol.

Guarding and feeding them was costing lots of money.

Lister had been quite clear at their last meeting.

King Manaccan was *very* unhappy about the cost of the prisoner accommodation...

...and the food bill was absolutely enormous.

These escalating costs were creating a huge, gaping hole in the Royal Coffers.

Scurvy had therefore started to become very worried about the pressing prisoner problem.

Then, one particularly dull and overcast morning, he received the news he'd been waiting for...

The Guillotine of Sirap was finally on board a ship...

...and bound for Wonrekland.

ONE HUNDRED & FOURTEEN

The Guillotine of Sirap

The Guillotine of Sirap had arrived on a ship from Ecnarf at Falmouth Port.

On the instructions of Major Merrymeet, Joharvy Par was watching everything that was going on at the port.

The state-of-the-art execution machine was so big that it had been taken apart for transportation. Mr Scurvy was overseeing the reassembly on the dock.

The contraption had a sturdy wooden platform as a base, with four wheels for moving it around.

Firstly, two long, wooden posts were dropped vertically into specially made holes in the base. Each of the posts had a slot gouged down one of its sides.

The workers put one of the posts in the wrong way.

'No, no,' said Scurvy, 'the slots need to face each other... on the *inside*... so that the blade can run up and down them.'

After putting the post back in the right way, the men picked up a flat piece of wood about the size of a small tabletop. Joh guessed it was about three feet square, and about three inches thick.

The square of wood had a hole in the middle about the diameter of a large human neck.

The men raised it all the way to the top of the two vertical posts and slid it down between the slots so that it rested on the platform at the bottom.

Mr Scurvy got up on to the platform, took hold of the square piece of wood, and pulled it upwards so that it came apart in the middle. The top half of the square in Scurvy's hand was now a rectangle with a semi-circular shape cut out of it. The bottom part had also become a rectangle with a semi-circular shape cut out of it.

Smsh!

Scurvy slammed his arm down so that the two halves of wood came together with a smash.

'Clever, isn't it?' he smirked to the workers.

'Any size head will fit in there.'

'Mmblmmblmmbl.'

The men mumbled an unenthusiastic reply. They knew that any one of their necks might be resting in that hole for the slightest misdemeanour.

Now the huge blade of the guillotine was unloaded.

It took four men to carry it.

The blade had a flat end and a slanted end.

The flat end was thick and heavy.

The slanted end was thin and sharp.

The four men used stepladders to raise the blade into the air and fitted it into the slots on the two vertical posts, with the sharp, slanted end pointing down.

Very gently, and very slowly, the men let the huge blade slide down between the slots, taking great care not to get their fingers or toes in the way of the slanted, slicing edge.

The big razorblade slid right down inside the three-inch thick wooden square.

Now Joh could no longer see through the circular hole because the metal blade was filling it.

A cross-beam was now rested on top of the two posts, and securely screwed in place.

Then a strong rope was threaded through the hole in the middle of the cross-beam, so that its two ends were hanging vertically down.

One of Scurvy's henchmen, complete with black uniform and Evstika, stepped forward, grabbed hold of one end of the rope, put it through the metal ring on top of the blade, and tied a strong knot.

The blade was finally ready to be raised.

A large crowd had been gathering to watch the arrival and assembly of the killing contraption.

'Ladies and gentlemen,' said Scurvy, obviously enjoying playing to the crowd.

'This is the Guillotine of Sirap...

The ultimate in modern execution technology.'

'Murmurmurmurmurmur.'

The crowd murmured nervously amongst themselves.

'Now for the test,' said Scurvy to the assembly, as he picked up a huge marrow that he had brought along especially for the purpose.

Very slowly and deliberately, he raised the top of the square piece of wood and rested the marrow in the semicircle in the bottom piece of wood.

'Imagine, if you will, that this is the neck of a rebel or a troublemaker.'

He then slammed down the top so that the marrow was trapped, with half sticking out at the front and half sticking out at the back.

'All we have to do to rid ourselves of them is this...'

With that, the Chief of Police gave the order.

'Guillotine UP!'

The henchman obeyed, pulling hand over hand on the other end of the rope.

The sharp heavy blade was drawn up into the air between the vertical posts, where it hung ominously as a hush fell over the watching crowd.

'Spread the word, good people,' said the Superintendent.

'Scurvy's Razor has arrived...

'All rebels and troublemakers had better watch out!'

He then gave another order.

'Guillotine DOWN!'

Slsssss!

'Ohhhhhhhhhhh!'

The crowd gasped as Scurvy's Razor sliced through the marrow like a surgeon's scalpel.

Thmp!

Half the marrow dropped into the basket at the front of the killing contraption with an awful thumping sound.

Scurvy raised the sliced marrow from the basket and held it aloft.

Still holding up the marrow for all to see, he smirked triumphantly at the crowd with a crooked smile as a stream of blood ran down his chin and dripped on to the platform.

It was at that moment that the Chief of Police noticed Joh taking an interest.

'What are you doing, boy?

'Nothing, sir, just watching.'

'Why aren't you in school?

'It started again last week, didn't it?'

Joh coughed the best coughing fit he could manage before replying in a spluttering voice.

'Very sick, sir.'

'Well, get back home then and mind your own business,' said Scurvy.

'Or do you want to be the first to try my new toy?'

'Yes, sir... I... I... mean, no, sir,' stuttered Joh, as he hurried away to report back to the Major.

ONE HUNDRED & FIFTEEN

The Conquest Colosseum

The Grand Colosseum of Emor had been constructed, a long time ago, as a centrepiece for the capital city of Evile's Empire.

The huge stadium, providing seating for a hundred thousand people, was famous for hosting great spectacles of entertainment called, 'Gladiator Games'.

It was an amazing feat of engineering. Thousands of combatants were kept below the stadium until called upon to fight. The whole floor of the stadium could even be flooded to recreate sea battles for the people to watch.

Throughout the Empire, the citizens loved to watch Gladiator Games. Evile wanted to keep the people happy. If they had their games, they wouldn't be too interested in what he was doing.

So the Emperor ordered the building of smaller colosseums all around the Empire. Some were simple stockades made of wood. Others were much bigger affairs made of stone.

On the orders of the Emperor, the Conquest Colosseum in Wonrekland was to be based on the Grand Colosseum. This would make it one of the Empire's most spectacular stadiums outside of Emor. The Conquest Colosseum would thus be a fitting commemoration of his victory over the kingdom that had been a thorn in his side for so long.

Although it was a much smaller version of the Emor stadium, the Conquest Colosseum was nevertheless going to be a very impressive venue.

Manaccan the Merciless was very pleased that its construction was going to schedule.

But the Emperor's Victory Visit was growing ever more imminent, and the King wanted everything to be just right.

Fortunately, the Emperor's Champion, Og the Ogreman, was already in Wonrekland and in training for his bout. That would bring in big crowds and get everything off to a good start.

However, Manaccan was aware of something very important in relation to the Gladiator Games: a steady supply of gladiators, animals, and creatures was required to fight in them if the event was to be rated as a success.

He had heard reports of other kings putting on very poor shows for the Emperor due to a lack of exciting combatants.

The King had therefore instructed his team to bring in the best gladiators they could find from around the Empire to fight in the colosseum, as well as boat-loads of strange animals and ferocious mutants to thrill the crowds.

He had also had to send a stiff reminder, with a copy of *Edict Number X*, to the eight Warlords. They had been slow to comply at first but had now each provided the required number of 'volunteer' gladiators from their respective Regions.

All this meticulous planning meant that, as the date of the Victory Visit approached, more and more gladiators, strange animals, and fearsome creatures were arriving by the day at ports in Wonrekland. This pleased Manaccan greatly.

He was determined this was going to be a games that Erthwurld would remember.

ONE HUNDRED & SIXTEEN

Scurvy's Sinister Solution

Scurvy's sinister solution to his prisoner problem was simple.

Now that the guillotine had arrived, he could start cutting off heads and the gaol would be empty in no time.

Once it had been constructed at the docks, the guillotine had been rolled into position in the central square at Nimdob.

This pleased Scurvy enormously for a number of reasons.

Firstly, it was very near the gaol, so there would be relatively little cost in transporting the prisoners to their place of execution. In fact, he had decided they could walk.

Secondly, Nimdob was right in the centre of Wonrekland. It was a very busy market town which meant that the executions would draw huge crowds to watch, and word would spread quickly that rebellion was highly dangerous.

Thirdly, he could see the huge sloping razor from his headquarters window in the square. He wouldn't even have to leave his office to watch the hourly executions.

Scurvy had also had another meeting with Lister, where an additional solution to the prisoner problem had just presented itself. King Manaccan wanted to make the first Emperor's Games in the Conquest Colosseum as spectacular as possible for the Victory Visit. The King had given his instructions. One in ten of the prisoners was to be trained as a gladiator.

The prisoners would draw lots. Most would get the Guillotine. The rest would have to fight.

ONE HUNDRED & SEVENTEEN

GUILTY!

Louis was so thirsty by the time they arrived at the newly named Wonrek Castle that his tongue felt like it was swollen and stuck to the roof of his mouth.

'Get him out of there, quickly,' said the officer in charge. 'He's to be taken straight to the court.'

As Louis was dragged along, one of the guards told him that the feelings against him in Wonrekland for what he did to the former King and Queen were so strong that he was being taken to a specially convened court for an immediate trial.

In the courtroom, King Manaccan sat in a big chair to one side whilst Louis faced the judge.

'The charges against you are these...' began an official-looking person in the court.

Louis was not allowed to speak to defend himself. And there was only one witness against him... Manaccan! So it was hardly surprising that, within a few minutes, the judge – who had been appointed specially by the new King – banged his gavel for the judgement: 'GUILTY!'

The judge then put a black cap on his head before pronouncing sentence in a very grave and sombre tone: 'Prince Louis of Forestland, owing to the callous and heinous nature of your crimes, it is the decision of this court that you shall henceforth be taken from this place to a place of execution... and there your head shall be separated from your body... by the Guillotine of Sirap.'

ONE HUNDRED & EIGHTEEN

Teachers In Trouble

The teachers were crammed together in two cells in Nimdob Gaol, men in one, women in the other.

Having survived the Towan Blystra Primary School bombing and narrowly missed being eaten by the hungry trog, Miss Perfect had gone back to work, only to find herself arrested in the middle of a lesson, along with all the other teachers.

The children had been very distressed to see their favourite teachers taken away.

They were even more distressed when they met the nasty teachers that Wendron had chosen.

Miss Prudent was standing next to Miss Perfect.

The elderly headmistress had been due to retire at the end of the year.

She was now very tired from having to stand all day and night in the prison cell.

The gaoler arrived and held out a clenched hand filled with straws.

'Right, it's time to draw lots.

'Long straws get the guillotine...

'Short straws get the colosseum.'

ONE HUNDRED & NINETEEN

Gnomes Incarcerated

The gnomes were incarcerated in a very small, cramped cell in Nimdob Gaol.

Prickle was not at all impressed.

'This really is too much,' she kept saying. 'It's filthy. Don't they ever sweep up in here?'

'I hope my plants are okay,' said Greenfingers. 'Those new seedlings will die without water.'

Seesaw and Swinger were missing the Playing Place.

'Eeewwwww.'

Dribble whimpered like a puppy. He was locked in his own tiny cage kennel in the corner of the same cell. He had no room to turn around. All the gnomes felt very sorry for him.

One morning, Ratphael arrived with a note.

King Manaccan had received special orders from the Emperor. His Imperiousness, who, for reasons unknown, hated all gnomes with a vengeance, had personally decided the fate of the gnomes of Washaway Wood.

The dungeoneer said nothing as he dropped the parchment through the bars and walked off down the corridor.

Plumper read the note to his friends.

'We aren't going to be allowed to draw lots like the other prisoners.

'They're going to make us fight in the colosseum...

'And we have to fight *each other*.'

ONE HUNDRED & TWENTY

Lots Of Anguish

The teachers were drawing lots in Nimdob Gaol.

There was great anguish amongst them as they each stepped forward to make their choice.

They didn't want to die.

They just wanted to teach.

But this was Wonrekland, where Evile's Terror now reigned.

Miss Perfect's fate was sealed when she pulled a very long straw.

She would face the Guillotine of Sirap.

Miss Prudent's fate, on the other hand, was almost certainly worse than the quick death offered by Scurvy's Razor.

She had drawn a short straw.

This meant the former headmistress would now be trained as a gladiator…

...to fight for her life in the Conquest Colosseum.

ONE HUNDRED & TWENTY-ONE

Major Merrymeet

Joh Par arrived at Trerice House just as Major Merrymeet and his wife were finishing their dinner.

He reported all that he had seen at Falmouth Port.

'So, the Guillotine of Sirap has arrived,' said the Major. 'Which makes it all the more important that we rescue your parents and the other teachers from the gaol as soon as possible.'

Joh didn't need reminding that his parents, both primary school teachers, had been in prison since Miss Wendron had been made Regulator of Schools. He had also read in the newspaper that the teachers were all either going to have their heads chopped off with the guillotine or be sent to fight as gladiators in the Conquest Colosseum.

'But how are we going to rescue them, Major?' asked Joh, with great concern.

'I cannot tell you the plan,' said Major Merrymeet. 'If you are captured and interrogated, it's best that you know nothing.'

What the major couldn't tell Joh was that he was a member of RAE and had already made contact with other members of the resistance. A plan had been set in motion to rescue the teachers, soldiers, and other innocent prisoners from Nimdob Gaol.

'From now on you'll have to stay inside,' decided Mrs Merrymeet. 'You're an only child and under twelve so you'll be on the slavers list. We can't risk you being taken.'

ONE HUNDRED & TWENTY-TWO

Guillotine or Gladiator?

Pemberley and Mrs Portwrinkle were talking in loud whispers again.

There was some measure of disagreement between them.

'Prince Louis has been sentenced to have his head chopped off at noon tomorrow,' said the cook in a very sombre tone. 'So, there's absolutely no chance of him surviving if that happens, is there?'

'I suppose not,' said the butler, 'but at least it's quick and humane. One slice and it's done. If he goes into the colosseum, as you suggest, he could take much longer to die. And his death might be horrible.'

'But if he fights as a gladiator, at least the boy will have a chance,' retorted Mrs Portwrinkle. 'And the games won't start for a couple of weeks, because the Conquest Colosseum isn't finished yet and they have to wait for the Emperor to arrive.'

'Yes, I see,' agreed Pemberley, 'so we would buy some time as well.'

'Precisely,' said Mrs Portwrinkle. 'If we don't try something like this, they'll have Prince Louis lying under that big razor and his head in the basket within twenty-four hours.'

'That settles it,' said Pemberley decisively.

'I'll talk to the King.'

ONE HUNDRED & TWENTY-THREE

We'll Stick With The Guillotine

The morning after his discussion with Mrs Portwrinkle, whilst dressing King Manaccan, Pemberley raised the subject of the condemned boy prince.

'I hope you don't mind my saying, Your Majesticness, but I was told the result of the trial of that traitorous young prince and I wondered if, perhaps, now that you have shown how wise and just you are by giving him a trial, it might give the people some satisfaction to see him fight and die in the colosseum.'

Pemberley could see that Manaccan was thinking hard about this suggestion, so he pushed a little harder.

'After all, the Guillotine of Sirap is so quick and it would all be over in a moment. That would hardly satisfy the people.'

'Yes, but we'd be certain to be rid of the little troublemaker,' said Manaccan.

'I think we'll stick with the Guillotine.'

ONE HUNDRED & TWENTY-FOUR

A Spectacular Death

'Of course, you do have a point there, Your Majesticness,' said Pemberley, as he desperately tried to steer his conversation with King Manaccan in the right direction. 'The Guillotine of Sirap is indeed very quick and efficient.'

Racking his brains, the butler then suddenly thought of a different angle.

'But the Emperor does love to see famous criminals in the games. It always keeps the people happy. He might be very grateful to you for making Prince Louis a gladiator and giving the people the satisfaction of seeing the murderer of their former King and Queen fighting for his life.'

'Hmm, that's true,' said Manaccan. 'But I'm still not sure. Strange things can happen at the games when the people get excited and choose their favourites. The Emperor has granted freedom to worse villains than Prince Louis when they've won their bouts.'

Pemberley could see he was in danger of losing his chance to persuade the King.

He was clutching at straws.

Then, in desperation, he blurted out the first thing that came into his head without thinking about it properly.

'Of course, Your Majesticness, if you wanted to guarantee that Prince Louis has a spectacular death, you could arrange for him to fight the Emperor's Champion.'

ONE HUNDRED & TWENTY-FIVE

Tipi City

The *Questers* emerged from the Crystal Door, right in the middle of a ring of totem poles at the top of a hill.

Tizzie looked down the hill. On every side below them there were cone-shaped tents arranged in small groups, spreading out as far as the eye could see in every direction.

'Tipi City,' said Clevercloggs.

'There are hundreds of them,' said Tizzie aloud.

'Looks more like thousands,' said Jack.

'There are indeed *thousands* of them,' confirmed Clevercloggs. 'And you see that big one in the centre, it's called the Great Tipi… but most people know it as the *Powwow Tipi*.'

'That's where we're headed,' said Mr Sand.

'Let's just have a quick look at the map,' said Clevercloggs.

'Good idea,' said Mr Sand as he opened the parchment. The point of red light was now much brighter. And it was flashing.

'I'd imagine that means we're very close?' mused Clevercloggs.

'Yes, I'd agree that's most likely,' said Mr Sand, 'but how do we know where to loo...'

Suddenly, before Mr Sand could finish, a thin beam of red light shot like a laser from high up on one of the totem poles.

ONE HUNDRED & TWENTY-SIX

The Red Laser

The laser emanating from the totem pole shone onto Jack's chest, creating a little red dot right over his heart.

Instinctively, he tried to move out of the way. But wherever he dodged and darted, the thin beam of bright red light followed his movements, so it always pointed at his heart.

'Well, I never...' said Clevercloggs, smiling sagely as he spoke. 'You didn't need to find the Red Rainbow Crystal young man... it's found you!'

'The magic of Godolphin is truly a powerful thing indeed,' said Mr Sand, as he looked at the source of the light; a tiny red crystal set in the totem pole. 'We need a ladder.'

'Perhaps we don't,' said Jack, looking at Clevercloggs as he pointed his wand at the little red stone.

'*Men rudh omma dos.*'

With that, the red crystal fell from the pole and into Jack's open palm.

'*Red stone come here*, very good,' said Clevercloggs, nodding and grinning in appreciation of Jack's efforts.

Jack smiled back at him.

'You can be the Keeper of the Crystals', said Clevercloggs, as he handed Jack a pouch which he had taken from his Cleversack. 'Put the first crystal in this little bag. It can hang round your neck by the drawstring. Make sure you keep it safe and out of sight under your shirt.'

ONE HUNDRED & TWENTY-SEVEN

Wow! Eagleponies

Clevercloggs set off down the hill, using his sticks for balance. Mr Sand walked with the little gnome.

They seemed to be having a deep and serious conversation.

Kea, Jack, and Tizzie followed on behind.

Tizzie now saw a magnificent sight.

Over the eastern horizon, high in the sky, came a hundred or more giant flying animals, each flapping its long blackish-brown wings slowly and purposefully.

They seemed to be part bird and part horse.

As she watched, hundreds more of the same majestic animals came flying towards Tipi City over every other horizon.

Each bird-horse carried at least one rider on its back.

The whole sky was soon filled with the wonderfully graceful animals.

Tizzie had never seen anything like them before.

Jack whispered in awe, just loud enough so that Tizzie could hear.

'Wow! Eagleponies...'

ONE HUNDRED & TWENTY-EIGHT

Sky Panther

The eagleponies flapped their huge wings majestically in the sky. It was clear they were all flying towards Tipi City as the *Questers* walked briskly down the hill. As the great skybeasts flew closer, Tizzie could see Redskins riding bareback on some of them. The hill was high and the *Questers* were only halfway down it when a group of the giant bird-horses flew overhead. The lead rider had a bow. He was aiming it straight at them!

'Look out!' warned Jack, 'he's going to fire at us.'

'Nothing to worry about,' said Clevercloggs nonchalantly. 'Sky Panther is a frien....'

Fmpp! An arrow suddenly thudded into the ground, less than a toe's width from Cleverclogg's right foot.

'And luckily he's a very good shot!' grinned Mr Sand.

There was a note attached to the arrow. Clevercloggs removed it and read its contents aloud.

'*Hello Old Friend, Long time, no see. You and your companions are very welcome. See you in the GT.*'

'What's a GT?' asked Tizzie.

'Oh that's just short for Great Tipi,' said Mr Sand.

Tizzie watched the eagleponies land in a clearing amongst the pointed tents as the *Questers* quickened their pace towards the largest of them.

More were flying in from every direction by the minute.

ONE HUNDRED & TWENTY-NINE

A Gathering Of Rebels

Redskin chiefs representing all the tribes of Acirema North were arriving on eagleponies from every direction and over every horizon.

From the north came the chiefs of the Blackfoot, Chinook, Sioux, and Crow.

From the south came the Comanche, Arapaho, Chickasaw, and Cheyenne.

From the east came the Cherokee, Iriquois, Creek, Delaware, and Shawnee.

And from the west came the Pomo, Chumash, Navajo, Hopi, Mohave, and Tillamook.

As well as Redskins, the eagleponies were bringing the leaders of settlers from all over Acirema North to Tipi City for the Great Powwow.

It was the greatest gathering of rebels that Erthwurld had ever seen.

Bella had flown in with Admiral Crumplehorn and other officers from the Land, Sea, and Air Guardians of Kernow.

The Kernish had been very surprised to learn that Chief Powhatan had arranged for sufficient skymounts to be available to transport himself and his daughter, as well as a number of representatives of the Kernish forces, to Tipi City.

Bella had been very excited to see the eagleponies arrive in the forest north of Enwotsemaj at the end of the secret meeting with Powhatan.

Her initial excitement had, however, soon turned into nervous anticipation when it came to actually *getting on* an eaglepony. She was a nautical warrior and, as such, was not at all accustomed to, or comfortable with, flying.

Cule, on the other hand, had won the high altitude aerobatics championship in Kernowland the previous year, on a racing chough called, 'Chaser'. So he absolutely loved flying, and, unlike his girlfriend, he had been very pleased to see the eagleponies arrive in the forest clearing on Netats Island.

After long flights, Cule and Bella had landed in Tipi City at almost exactly the same time.

ONE HUNDRED & THIRTY

Together Again

It was as if fate had played a helping hand when Bella and Cule bumped into each other in the food tent.

They were both trying to grab something to eat before the Great Powwow started.

Words could not describe how pleased they were to see each other.

They hugged and kissed and each told the other the tale of how they had come to be in Tipi City.

Then, forgetting for a moment who and where they were, they held hands as they made their way into the Great Tipi.

A look from Admiral Crumplehorn was enough to make them think better of such a public display of affection.

They quickly separated and took their seats in the big tent to await the start of the powwow.

ONE HUNDRED & THIRTY-ONE

The Great Tipi

Tizzie thought the Great Tipi was even bigger than the circus tent she had been to with Mum and Dad and Louis last year.

Thoughts of her family made her a little sad but she was soon brought back to the moment by the sight that greeted her as she followed the others into the tipi.

In the centre there was a ring of bare ground. Just like the circus tent, thought Tizzie. In the middle of the ring was a circular leather mat which was about three paces across.

Around the ring of bare ground, there were rows of bench seats going backwards and upwards in concentric circles. Almost every seat was taken.

Outside the tent they had heard no noise, but, strangely, inside, the sound of voices was almost deafening.

Cleverclоggs seemed to know where he was going. He made his way towards a seat right in the front row with his name on it. Tizzie went to follow him.

'No, no, no,' said Mr Sand, gently. 'I'm afraid we aren't on the Inner Circle of Representatives. We're just guests.'

They were soon sitting in the visitor seats, high in the stands.

'Looks like there are representatives from all the tribes from every corner of Acirema North,' said Mr Sand. 'And there's William Smith, the leader of the western settlers. They must have agreed to be represented here too.'

ONE HUNDRED & THIRTY-TWO

Chiefs Of The Tribes

Mr Sand now pointed around the Inner Circle, showing Kea, Jack, and Tizzie who was who amongst the chiefs of the tribes, rebel leaders, and other important people.

'You know the clever old gnome. On his left is Standing Bear, then Black Hawk – a fearsome brave. Next is Sequoia. Then the old man is Sitting Bull. The even older man on his left is Hiawatha. As the most senior chief, he'll lead the Great Powwow Ceremony. Sky Panther is next to him, then Geronimo, and then Pontiac.

'Next is William Smith, we've already mentioned him. Then Brendan Blarney, the leader of the settlers in the east. That woman there is Sacajawea; she heads a tribe where the men and women share all the jobs – cooking, cleaning, hunting… and fighting too.'

Tizzie was struck by how magnificent the Redskin chiefs looked, all sitting next to each other in the Inner Circle, dressed in their feather headdresses and colourful, ceremonial clothes.

Mr Sand came to the end of his pointing.

'And that's Crazy Horse, then Squanto, then Cochise… and finally, next to Clevercloggs, is his good friend, Chief Powhatan.'

Drm, drm, drm, drm.

Drm, drm, drm, drm.

Suddenly, there was a beating of drums as Hiawatha stood up and made his way into the ring.

ONE HUNDRED & THIRTY-THREE

The Rippling Rising Mat

Hiawatha stopped at the edge of the circular mat and addressed the Inner Circle.

'Chiefs of the Tribes, we are gathered for a Great Powwow. The most important meeting we have ever attended. By tradition, as Senior Elder, I call upon the ancestors to join us to offer wisdom and guidance.'

With that, Hiawatha closed his eyes, held out his arms to either side, and began chanting under his breath.

'Haiyaiyaiya haiyaiyah. Haiyaiyaiya haiyaiyah.'

A tingle went through Tizzie's body and the hairs on the back of her neck began to stand up.

All the other chiefs sitting in the Inner Circle now stood up and joined in the chanting.

'Haiyaiyaiya haiyaiyah.'

The circular mat in the centre of the ring began to ripple as if a slow wave were moving through it. Now all the other Redskins in the Great Tipi stood up and chanted loudly.

'HAIYAIYAIYA HAIYAIYAH.'

'HAIYAIYAIYA HAIYAIYAH.'

The sides of the Great Tipi began to ripple.

'HAIYAIYAIYA HAIYAIYAH.'

Tizzie was enthralled as her gaze was drawn to the rippling mat.

'HAIYAIYAIYA HAIYAIYAH.'

The mat was rising off the ground on its own!

ONE HUNDRED & THIRTY-FOUR

The Crystal Well

The mat rose higher and higher into the air.

It reached the head of the chanting chief and carried on, higher and higher, and higher still, as the chanting continued.

Suddenly, as the mat reached the apex of the Great Tipi and floated there in mid-air, the chanters stopped, all at once.

There was silence for what seemed like ages.

Tizzie daren't ask the question that was on her lips.

Jack spoke in a whisper.

'Wow! The *Crystal Well.*'

'Shhh!' admonished Mr Sand.

Now revealed on the ground, where the mat had been, was a circle of crystal.

It was like the Crystal Pool, but much larger, and it seemed to be made of clear crystal.

It twinkled like a diamond.

Although it was solid crystal, it gave the impression of being a deep well.

'What's it for?' asked Tizzie.

'You'll soon see,' said Mr Sand.

'Now, no more talking please.

'Just watch and listen.'

ONE HUNDRED & THIRTY-FIVE

Lone Eagle

After the interminable period of silence, the Crystal Well began to ripple. It was no longer solid, but it wasn't quite liquid either.

Tizzie was even more enthralled.

Now the rippling waves became all the colours of the rainbow. First there were red waves, which were soon joined by orange waves, and then yellow waves; until seven different colours of wave were mixing together.

Then clouds of rainbow coloured mist rose up from the Crystal Well and swirled around above it.

Suddenly, seven coloured beams shot into the air from the centre of the crystal and merged together to form one white beam of light.

A figure began to form inside the beam.

Then, suddenly, the beam was gone.

A man was standing in its place.

But he wasn't solid, like a real person, and he wasn't just a picture. He was a mix of the two.

Tizzie thought he looked a bit like the hologram she had seen at the Science Museum.

The figure raised his hand in greeting.

He spoke softly.

It was as if Tizzie could hear his voice in her ears, but also inside her head.

'I am Lone Eagle, a Guardian of The One Light.'

ONE HUNDRED & THIRTY-SIX

Programme Of Dread

Most of those who were going to fight in the Gladiator Games were filled with dread at the prospect.

The *Programme of Colosseum Events* was published some time in advance of the games.

Posters had gone up all over Wonrekland advertising the forthcoming contests.

Scurvy had helpfully sent a copy of the programme to Nimdob Gaol, so the prisoners who had drawn the short straws could see who they were matched with.

Plumper was reading the programme to the other gnomes.

'We're all on here, under a special section called *Gladiator Gnomes*.

Prickle v Flowerpot

Plumper v Longlegs

Swinger v Seesaw

Greenfingers v Fishalot

'And Dribble has to fight too…

Dribble the Dachshund v Danglefang the Wolfspider

'And there are all sorts of other bouts like…

Headmistress Prudent v Chomp the Chewing Chihuahua

Lieutenant Liskeard v Cyco the Sumo Cyclops

'And,' concluded Plumper, after reading out the whole list of events, 'that young prince who killed the King and Queen is topping the bill against the Emperor's Champion.'

All the other gnomes now peered over to look at the main gladiator bout on the programme:

Prince Louis
the Boy Assassin

versus

Og the Ogreman

- NEXT -

After reading, *Slavechildren*, the fifth book in the Kernowland series, you may want certain questions answered:

Will Tizzie and the other *Questers* be able to find *Photos* and all seven of the Rainbow Crystals?

Can Jack learn to wield the *Amulet of Hope* and produce the Bright Beam against the evil Forces of Darkness?

Why has Lone Eagle appeared in the Crystal Well?

Will Louis be smashed into little pieces by Og's ironhammer in the Conquest Colosseum?

Will Miss Prudent, the Headmistress, be torn limb from limb by Chomp the Chewing Chihuahua?

Will the gnomes be made to fight each other to the death?

Will Dribble be devoured by Danglefang?

If so, you may get some answers by reading Book 6, the next title in the exciting Kernowland series:

Kernowland 6 Colosseum of Dread

Visit our websites for up-to-date information about new titles, publication dates, and popular school visits by the author

www.kernowland.com
www.erthwurld.com

ERTH
GLACIERLAND
WILDLAND
ACIREMA NORTH
The Revenger
LAKELAND
PRARIELAND
Tizzie
Ratlarbig Rock
Port of Acnalbasac
Isles of Airanac
CIFICAP OCEAN
QUAKELAND
SWAMPLAND
Abuc
CAVELAND
Port Lujnab
CITNALTA OCEAN
RIVERLAND
ACIREMA SOUTH
MOUNTAINLAND
Cap'n Pigleg of TheRevenger
N
W
E
S